Sherlock Holmes:
Eliminate the Impossible

by Paula Hammond

Edited by David Marcum

All characters appearing in this work are fictitious. Any resemblance to real persons, living or dead, is purely coincidental. The opinions expressed herein are those of the author and not of MX Publishing.

Hardcover ISBN 978-1-80424-406-7
Paperback ISBN 978-1-80424-407-4
ePub ISBN 978-1-80424-408-1
PDF ISBN 978-1-80424-409-8

Published by MX Publishing
335 Princess Park Manor, Royal Drive,
London, N11 3GX
www.mxpublishing.com

Cover design by Nusrat Abbas Awan

Table of Contents

The Bleeding Heart Mystery

Holmes was lounging on the sofa, his tall, spare form swaddled in a purple dressing gown, his long, thin hands moving with grace and precision. I'm no musician, but I didn't need my companion's unique skills to guess that he was replaying, in his mind's-eye, Sarasate's *Zigeunerweisen*, which we had heard performed at St. Johns' Square the previous evening.

In such reveries, Holmes was no longer the man I had so often caricatured in my case notes. Instead, his keen features were transformed. With eyes closed and a gently smiling face he was, at that moment, at the zenith of the metronome's swing. I knew that, in an instant, the pendulum could swing back and my dear friend would once again be the determined sleuth-hound of fond acquaintance.

"My dear Watson" he said, lazily, "do be seated. Mrs. Hudson has been in a whirl all morning, and should you continue to lurk in the doorway I fear she will be compelled to sweep you up."

I'd often heard Holmes's clients tell their extraordinary stories, but now that I was possessed of a tale of my own, I found it wasn't such an easy task. So there I remained, paused on the threshold, contemplating how best to broach the subject.

Something about my inaction caught Holmes's interest and he bolted upright, every inch the detective once again. "I take it from your attitude that this morning's excursion to Leather Lane was more fruitful than you'd hoped?"

I'd risen early and left our rooms while Holmes was still asleep. I certainly hadn't mentioned any appointments. It was true that, by now, I was used to such remarkable pronouncements from my friend, but my amazement remained.

"I honestly have no idea how you deduced that," I exclaimed to Holmes's evident delight.

"Ah, Watson! The notes on today's expedition are written very clearly. You are, as I'm sure you'd agree, a creature of habit. You generally do your rounds on foot, leaving and returning at much the same time every day. In the evening, you polish your shoes and lay out your bag, ready for the next day. Today you rose early, and leaving your bag behind, took a hansom to Leather Lane."

"But – " I began.

"Your shoes" Holmes chuckled. "They still have their shine. And, as to the location – well that handkerchief you keep in your sleeve, in fine military style, shows traces of mustard. Put that together with the sesame seed on your collar, and I'd hazard you've partaken of a breakfast of that famed Yiddish delicacy, a salt beef beigel. A speciality of Leather Lane eateries."

"I admit to everything you say. But you couldn't possibly know my frame of mind."

"Oh, come, you do me a disservice." Holmes exclaimed, clearly enjoying every moment. "I would be a poor companion if I hadn't noticed your prolonged silences. Your sighs. The well-thumbed text books. You've been vexed by a problem, and it's not too much of a leap to believe that this morning's unusual expedition has something to do with it. Now, my dear fellow, pull up a chair and don't keep me in suspense any longer."

I did as instructed and, in our customary positions, with Holmes on one side of the fireplace and I on the other, I began.

"You've heard, no doubt, of the great American inventor, Dodson Hughes?"

"The whole world surely knows that gentleman's name." Holmes said. "Don't tell me he's a patient?"

"Not exactly. This isn't widely known, for fear of spooking his shareholders, but for the past year Hughes been suffering from increasingly severe bouts of bronchitis. I have a young patient similarly afflicted and I had, in truth, begun to despair of ever finding a treatment which would ease her distress. A few days ago, an old friend from my Barts days mentioned that Hughes was rumored to be working on a new inhalation device. Now, it sounds like pure quackery. Even if he has been haunting the lecture halls, the man has no medical training. But it's a terrible thing to watch a child fade before your eyes and feel helpless to stop it, so I determined to see Hughes and this miracle device of his."

"He lives in the country, does he not?" Holmes asked, his interest piqued.

"West Norwood, I believe, but his workshops are in Hatton Garden, and he commutes to the City regularly to supervise the work. As you know, most of Hatton Gardens' businesses are diamond cutters and jewelry-makers. Visitors are strictly forbidden and, given the nature of Hughes' work, he adheres to the same rules as his neighbors, so that all business meetings are conducted in local cafés."

"Hence the beigel?"

“Indeed.”

“And his inhalation device?”

“Still in development, he said. But you’ll be amused to know that he calls it his ‘Peace Pipe’! It is only right that after creating so many murderous machines, he should do something to try and save lives. It will, I think, be some time before it enters production and he was violently protective of its secrets. However . . . .”

“That isn’t what brought you to rushing back to Baker Street with mustard on your whiskers?”

“No,” I laughed. “That was something infinitely stranger.”

Sandwiched between Kings Cross and Farringdon, Hatton Garden is one of London’s few remaining villages. No doubt its cobbled byways, timber-framed buildings, and tightly-packed lanes will soon be brushed away, as the city continues to replace wood with stone, quaint beauty with brash commerce. But, for now, this Medieval remnant clings determinedly on. Indeed, just as Scotland Yard once belonged to the kings of Scotland, this part of London once belonged to the Bishops of Ely, and is still technically, if not actually, in Cambridgeshire.

It was the great Tudor queen, Elizabeth, who grabbed part of the Bishop’s estate for one of her favorites, Sir Christopher Hatton. Down a narrow alley, hidden behind rows of marble-fronted homes, still stands the tiny tavern where the young princess is said to have danced around a cherry tree in the courtyard one May morning. Walk down Ely Place, past the church where Henry and Catherine of Aragon famously feasted, and you enter Bleeding Heart Yard – a warren of dark backstreets that will, with many twists, turns, and dead ends, eventually lead you to Leather Lane. It was there, in a cozy corner of a kosher café, that my tale began.

As I spoke, Holmes leant forward, regarding me with eyes kindled. It was unusual to find myself on the receiving end of such fevered scrutiny and I must admit, it wasn't an all-together comfortable experience.

Fifty-years of age, with a shock of snow-white hair and an overgrown Van Dyke beard to match, Dodson Hughes was a man in whom passions ran deep. Several times during our interview he accused me of trying to steal his secrets. It was only when I'd shared my own researches into the bronchial disease that afflicted him that he visibly relaxed – realizing, perhaps, that I could provide the expertise he lacked. However, our interview had barely begun when the day took a distinct turn for the bizarre.

The café door flew open and a small, red-haired man, blanched with terror, gave a strangled yell and fairly fell across the threshold.

He was gathered up and deposited at a spare table with all the efficacy you'd expect from an establishment that serves all-day breakfasts to the hurried and the hungry. I rose to offer my services, for he was much excited, with the sort of wide-eyed near-hysteria I'd often seen in those who've endured a sudden shock.

"She's back!" he whispered "Back . . . with death at her heels!" The café fell silent. A small clique had gathered around the table, but now, even those who'd remained seated turned to regard the agitated speaker.

"There! There in the Yard! Drenched in blood!" he sobbed, his voice cracking. "There will be death. Mark my words! Death!" And with that final cry, he fell into a dead faint.

A waft of smelling salts brought him round and a small brandy did the rest, but the fellow was a mess – sweaty-faced, pale, trembling, and clearly embarrassed to have made such a spectacle of himself. Indeed, no amount of cajoling could compel him to elaborate on his curious pronouncement.

Hughes dismissed the whole thing as occasioned by "too much drink and too little learning". The café owner spoke witheringly of "soft-brained men repeating tales told to keep children a-bed". The patrons returned to their business dealings and the whole thing was quickly brushed under the table.

"I naturally insisted on escorting my new patient to a cab and Hughes – irritable at the interruption – hastened off to his place of business in something of a funk. But there's a mystery here, Holmes! I can taste it."

Holmes raised his eyebrows. "The case does have some interesting elements. Yes. Very interesting . . . If you would permit me?"

He took hold of my left sleeve and proceeded to examine the cuff.

"This stain – was it here yesterday?"

"I hadn't noted it. Oil from the hansom's step, no doubt." I commented.

Holmes said nothing, but I could tell from the flush of his cheek that his keen mind had found something of interest in my curious tale.

"You think there's something in it?"

"Yes" Holmes said quietly. "I do."

"Off to Hatton Garden, then?" I hazarded.

"Naturally! Holmes chuckled. "Who am I to argue with a client? Especially when he also happens to be my dearest friend."

There's been a Bleeding Heart Tavern in Hatton Garden for at least four-hundred years. The current building is a mere one-hundred-and-fifty years old, but its small, round, sunken bar tells of an older history, and of one pub built on the ashes of another. The bricks and mortar may be Georgian, but the design testifies to a time when bears were baited in the pit while the patrons sat atop, drinking and laying bets. Today, it still has a bad reputation: "*Drunk for a penny. Dead drunk for two-penny*" was the disquieting boast emblazoned over the door.

We stepped down into the main bar and Holmes made a bee-line for a rickety table inhabited by a baby-faced man in worn tweed who had the look of one permanently delighted by the world.

Joseph March was what Holmes terms a "cultural historian", specializing in London's myths and legends. How he knew Holmes I never did discern, but then, given how reluctant my flat-mate could be to leave Baker Street at all, the fact that he knew anyone beyond myself and Mrs. Hudson was a source of constant surprise.

"Pleased to see my telegram reached you, Joe", Holmes began. "What do you have for me?"

"Well, Mr. 'Olmes, with your love of the grotesque, I'm surprised you don't already know the tale. It's about a murder too. Right up your street."

Holmes laughed heartily. "Ah, Joe, but you're the expert. Please. Watson and I are all ears."

"Well, you asked if there might be any tales about the area that could account for the good doctor's curious experience. Truth be told, it didn't take much digging. It's a fairly well-known tale, tho' the legend mixes things up a bit. In reality, the supposed victim – Lady Hatton – lived a long life, but of the fact that a murder took place here there's no doubt. Places don't get named Bleeding Heart Yard on a whim!"

March closed his eyes, lent back, and began to weave his tale, his tone, just as a story-teller's should be: Low, warm, and enticing.

"Now, this was in the time of good Queen Bess. Holborn Hill, on which we sit, was still an actual hill, with trees and pathways winding down towards the valley floor. Today that's where the viaduct stands, but back then you would have found the River Fleet. Today, that great waterway is nothing more than a boarded-over sewer, but then it was fast and deep enough for the Queen to sail her barge all the way up to the Clerkenwell. But some things haven't changed. This tavern was still a tavern, not long since built. And the courtyard outside was still a popular place for festivities. And this is where our story starts. In these streets, under these stars, but many, many lifetimes ago . . . ."

One evening, or so the story goes, Lady Hatton was hosting a feast. She was an ambitious lady, keen to impress the

Queen and the Court. Desperate, in fact. So desperate that she'd made a pact with the devil. In exchange for one glorious evening – a ball, the greatest names in the land in attendance – she would sell him her soul.

This was to be the evening. Everything would be perfect. Every dish, every drink, every moment. And at the centre of it all, there she would be. Stylish. Beautiful. The belle of the ball. At the end of the evening, it was promised, everyone would know her name. She would be the talk of London. Her future seemed assured, and all it would cost was something that she'd never seen and didn't believe in.

Fiddlers! Fiddlers! Fiddle away!
Resin your catgut! Fiddle and play!
A roundelay! A roundelay! A roundelay, I say!
Fiddle, fiddle, fiddle, away!

The musicians strike up a tune. The Lady opens her doors. And the ball begins.

And what a ball! It's like a waking dream. Live birds cut from the belly of a roasted boar whirl aloft, dropping gold leaves into the laps of the guests. Gem-encrusted tapestries glitter under the flickering candlelight. Jugglers and acrobats perform impossible feats. Dancers appear to walk on air. And everyone who is everyone is here.

As midnight approaches, the doors are thrown open once more and the musicians lead the guests out into the courtyard – the courtyard that's just outside this tavern. And as they dance and sing, a strange sound is heard. A deep clattering, like hooves running across the rooftops. But no matter. The party's in full flow and no one even notices the stranger who suddenly appears in their midst. At least, not at first.

Tall, dressed in black, he joins the dance, leaping, bounding into the courtyard. He throws himself into the air, pirouettes, lands with the surety of a cat, then leaps again. He leaps, he pirouettes, lands. Again. And again. The musicians take their cue from him. Faster and faster they play, their fingers getting bloody – seemingly unable to stop even if they'd wanted to.

Here's Lady Hatton, resplendent in white silk and ermine. He grasps her by the waist and springs into the air. Again, and again, and again. Lady Hatton is delighted. Swirling high over her guests' heads, she's laughing, gasping. She glances down and sees the party-goers begin to scatter. She turns, dizzy with exaltation, looks at her dance partner and finally sees what her guests have seen. The devil in all his satanic glory. His hands – claws. His feet – hooves. His face twisted into a wide, wide, smile and, on his head, a pair of vast horns, burning with the fires of damnation.

And the next morning, when the guests returned to see if what they had seen was a dream or not, what did they find? No signs of the sumptuous feast. No signs of the night's revels.

Of poor Lady Hatton, needless to say,
No traces of her have been found to this day,
Nor of the terrible dancer who whisk'd her away;
But out in the courtyard – and just in that part –
lay, throbbing and still bleeding: A Huge Human Heart!

It was just as March had concluded his tale – thumping the table and laughing heartily – that an eerie cry rocked the tavern. Holmes vaulted across the room and was at the door almost before the call had died out. I followed, fast on his heels, dreading, in the thrall of March's singular narrative, what we might find. We weren't disappointed. There, standing in the courtyard by the old water pump, was Lady Hatton herself. Her robes had once been white but now they were drenched in blood. A dark, gaping hole lay in her chest and in her hand she was holding her own heart. She looked at us, smiled with a sort of rapacious desperation, then threw the heart into the air. I scanned the dark sky, but could see nothing, and when I'd glanced back the Lady, too, had vanished.

We stood for some time in the chill air, considering this unexpected turn of events. Holmes said nothing, but in the half-light from the tavern's windows, I distinctly saw him smile.

Needless to say, news of the apparition spread quickly and, within the quarter-hour, the tavern was packed with locals jostling for position at the pewter-topped bar. With ale to loosen their tongues and lessen their fears, there was none of the reticence to speak that the patrons in the café had displayed. The talk was wild, and several times I overheard a newcomer loudly proclaiming that he'd "seen it all" while credulous onlookers *Ooh*-ed and *Ahh*-ed at his tale.

March was as giddy as a schoolboy, jogging from table to table, noting down every half-recalled tit-bit of "the Bloody

Lady" in a voluminous notebook. Holmes, no less intrigued, sat quietly, soaking it all up in his own inimitable way.

Eventually the crowds began to disburse and Holmes and I headed for Lincoln's Inn, where the small, green cabman's shelter would be sure to provide a driver looking for late-night trade.

The hansom dropped us at Baker Street just after midnight and, although the day had been long and wearying, I was too eager for Holmes's take on events to feel sleepy.

My companion ensconced himself in the fireside armchair, pulled a cigar from the coal scuttle, and began to puff complacently.

"Well?" I asked.

"Well, Watson?" he replied, grinning at my obvious impatience.

"Well?" I repeated.

Holmes glanced at me mischievously, and I feared we would spend the whole evening in a round-robin of "Wells", when he suddenly he slapped his thigh and burst into a paroxysm of amusement.

"Watson, this has, I think, been one of the most entertaining evenings I've had for many years!"

"Entertaining? Horrifying I would have said!" picturing the lady and her bloodied dress with a shudder.

"Oh, my dear doctor – "

"No, no" I interrupted, hotly, feeling more than a little chagrin at being the subject of so much levity. "I know the great Sherlock Holmes doesn't believe in ghosts – "

"Oh, no, Watson. Please forgive me!" Holmes composed himself. "My humor wasn't aimed at you. And as for whether or not I believe in ghosts, you know my techniques. I deal in facts, not faith. Should someone present me with unequivocal proof of the existence of ghosts, goblins, or even the Easter hare, then I would accept it wholeheartedly. No, as entertaining as this evening's events have been, that's all they've been. Entertainment. A distraction. And very well done it was too."

"But I saw – ?"

"You saw, but you didn't observe."

Holmes walked over to the scuttle, took out a fist-sized piece of coal, and began tossing it in the air. Higher and higher.

I watched intently as the small piece of carbon flew from Holmes's hand, into the air, then back again. "Now," Holmes said, "watch carefully." The coal vanished. I saw it leave his hand – thrown into the air – I would have sworn to it.

"But how?" I ejaculated.

"Simple" Holmes replied, pointing to the carpet where I could see that the coal now lay. "Your mind sees what it expects to see. It expected me to throw the coal, and the smallest movement of my hand was enough to persuade you that's what had happened. But, just like in the courtyard, it's classic misdirection."

"Everyone watches the heart, while the Lady makes her exit."

"Just so. But it's all been misdirection, don't you see? Everything. The piece of theatre in the café and tonight's materialization, everything. You recall that greasy-stain on your coat cuff? Almond oil and starch, I'd vouch – face cream and powder. The tools of the actor's trade. You did note how sweaty and pale the man appeared . . . ."

"But why?"

"Now that is the question. Who knew of your meeting with Hughes?"

"I'd written to his place of business several times before he granted me an interview."

"Did you specify why you wanted to meet?"

"I didn't feel it prudent to mention that his new project was being openly discussed. I merely noted that it might be mutually beneficial if we met.

"So it's possible that someone on his staff knew he would be meeting the renowned Dr. Watson of 221b Baker Street, for reasons of 'mutual benefit'."

I began to see where Holmes's train of thought was leading. "But this is all-too wonderful!" I exclaimed. "And the episode in the café . . . ."

"Presumably to stop whatever discussion it was imagined that Hughes and yourself might have."

"And tonight?"

"A piece of last-minute theatricals."

"You think that all this fuss has been to draw my – *our* – attention elsewhere?"

"I think, Watson, that's a question that will best be answered after a good night's sleep."

And with that Holmes retired to his bedroom, leaving me to stare into the fire and wonder.

Bleeding Hart Yard was as gloomy during the day as it had been the previous evening. The brick was dark – slick with grease and soot. The hustle and bustle of Leather Lane was just few streets away, but the close-packed buildings muffled all sound and overhung the narrow passage in a way that made the place eerily claustrophobic.

"March mentioned that the Fleet runs nearby," Holmes said, all the time talking to himself rather than to me. "This pump is rusted solid but doubtless drew water from the Fleet back in the day. Hmm, but now that venerable river has been repurposed, I'd wager that there's a manhole cover nearby. Ah, yes, yes. Here it is. Making a very handy getaway route for our Bloody Lady. And ha, ha! What have we here?"

He threw me an object, plucked from the ground, which proved to be a lump of shiny, red wax. The Lady's eviscerated heart!

"The joke of it is," he said "that it was the elaborate nature of the thing that aroused my interest. If it hadn't been for the command performance in the café, your meeting with Hughes would have been a footnote over morning coffee and toast."

As he spoke, his brows drew into two hard black lines, his eyes shining from beneath them with a steely glint. I saw him glance down at the manhole cover, then back up, seeming to scan the path that led from the courtyard to Leather Lane.

"Look here! It was dry yesterday evening, with a sudden downpour overnight. I'd not expected to find our Lady's footprints, but see this! Hobnails. And look how they've been smudged. The movement of manhole cover being dragged back into place. Someone has been here this very morning. Hmm. I wonder?"

Not for the first time in our long acquaintance, I was confused, and admitted as much.

For an answer Holmes gave a distracted nod. "You know, Watson, I think I may take a short constitutional. Care to join me? Oh, and if you would slip your revolver out of your pocket, I'd be very obliged."

With that, he hoisted off the manhole cover and threw himself into the dark void beneath.

The ladder complained bitterly as I climbed down. Its creaks and groans were such that they created the impression of an army of specters eagerly waiting in the oubliette below. I had to remind myself several times that everything we'd seen so far had been mere mummery.

I was a foot or two from the bottom when the fastenings finally gave way and I was forced to jump the remaining distance, landing hard on my game leg.

The ladder landed on top of me, adding insult to injury, and it took some time for Holmes to help me disentangle myself from the wreckage of rusted iron.

"Are you hurt?

"I'll live," I replied, gingerly testing my weight on my old war injury. It hurt like the blazes, but I was determined not to be the laggard.

Although the narrow tunnel curved above our heads, with many feet of London clay on top, we had no need for Holmes's flashlight. Besides, the dry cell batteries wouldn't last long and, for now, we were better off relying on the fat lamps someone had helpfully hung at intervals along the tunnel wall.

Holmes lit one and the flickering light revealed what he seemed to have already guessed. The route of the old River Fleet, culverted by brick, ran straight for a while, following the path of Gray's Inn Road, before curving down towards the Holborn Viaduct. But there was another passage, which had been roughly cut into the tunnel walls. The work looked to be old and I was reminded that every part of London has tales of such secret passageways. There had been a convent here once. Maybe these had been used by Catholics to escape the wrath of mad Queen Mary? Maybe they were built during the Civil War, or by rum smugglers? Or maybe to allow some rich Lord to visit his mistress unobserved. Who knew? But now . . . .?

Holmes had pulled one of the fat lamps from its sconce and we let its fitful light guide us. I could discern very little in the gloom, though I thought I heard noises ahead. We slowed, Holmes extinguished the light, and for a while we stood, crouched together, in that tomb of wet earth – listening. Yes! Without doubt: Voices.

We edged closer but, in my eagerness, I stepped without thought and my leg, still aching from my earlier tumble, gave way beneath me. I fell with a thud and this time it did not go unnoticed.

A shout. Feet cannon-balling on hard earth. Then, a sound that I shall take with me to my grave. The noise of a lever, much rusted, being thrown and, quick on its heels, a roar like thunder, as a large body of water – the run-off from the evening's storm, now channeled by some unseen force – began to race down the tunnel behind us. Good Lord! Someone had opened the sluice gates!

Holmes pulled me to my feet, but my leg buckled beneath me and I went down again. A rat brushed past my outstretched shoe. Another, then another followed, and as I struggled back onto my feet, I could hear their terrified squeals as they raced to escape the approaching torrent.

With Holmes near carrying me, we backtracked – by unspoken agreement, making for the little passageway we'd seen cut into the tunnel wall.

Even through the water was only still only ankle-deep, the force of its flow testified to the power of the oncoming deluge. Yet, it wasn't the water itself I feared – rather what it would bring with it. A fetid smell had begun to fill the tunnel, and I had in my mind the horrible deaths of the six-hundred-and-fifty people onboard the Princess Alice when it sank in the Thames. Not drowned, but burnt and suffocated by the raw sewage which had been flushed into the river, ready to be taken out by the tide.

Already I was gagging, my eyes beginning to sting, and I knew that should I smell the tell-tale rotten-egg scent of hydrogen sulfide we were dead men.

Finally, with cold fingers doing the work that our eyes couldn't, we found the entrance to the little passageway. Holmes hoisted himself up and I clambered after. I could still hear sounds in the tunnel ahead. For a second, the voices became louder, the footsteps panicked. Then, a cry, long and agonizing, was suddenly extinguished. It was that silence, I think, that spurred me on. The blood in my veins turned to ice, and I ran like the very devil himself was at my heels.

Holmes veered left, and left again, following some instinct or mental map – I knew not which. Dizzy with pain, I followed where he led. At some point he had clicked on his flashlight, but in my fever, I hadn't noticed until I saw his face in the strangely yellow and distorted glow of the bulls-eye lens, set in an attitude of grim determination.

“There!” He shone the electric torch and, ahead, I saw a little ladder leading up into a brick alcove. He helped me scramble up, following fast on my heels. In front of us was a small wooden door and there we crouched, hammering and hollering as though our very lives depended on it – which at that moment I truly believed they did.

It seemed to me that we spent hours hunkered there, in the dark, with the threat of certain death in every breath. Holmes turned his knuckles bloody with the force of his knocking and, in truth, I thought we were done for. Hoarse, frozen, and cramped, we had just decided to risk returning to the passageway when the hatch opened and a grizzled-faced man, spat, cursed, and hauled us out into the warmth of Dodson Hughes' machine room.

Hughes himself quickly appeared, red-faced and blustering at what he took to be thieves caught in the act of stealing secrets. Upon recognizing myself and, by association, Holmes, however, his attitude became one of studious attention.

“Why, I'd heard of the great Baker Street detective,” he said, “but I hadn't known he was psychic! Just this very morning I'd missed some vital documents and, having made the acquaintance of the good doctor, was on my way to consult with you.”

The grizzle-faced man busied around. Blankets and hot chocolate were procured and a place cleared for us by the little stove. There, Holmes – though much abused and still wan from our subterranean adventures – began to put together the missing parts of the puzzle.

“May I ask”, Holmes said “exactly what it is you’ve been working on?”

“A gun, Mr. Holmes. A gun like no other. Single-barrel, belt-fed, capable of six-hundred-and-sixty-six rounds a minute.”

Having seen what just one bullet could do to a man, there was something horrifying about the evident pride that Hughes took in his latest invention, but I held my peace.

“And these documents were plans for that gun? But if I’m not mistaken, you’ve missed them before, have you not?”

“Why yes!” Hughes replied, much amazed. “Played holy hell with the staff. Threatened to get the police involved. I was quite the tyrant for days afterwards!”

“Then they turned up mis-filed?”

“Exactly so!”

“And what about your visitors? The ones you’ve been lodging at the Bleeding Heart Tavern?” Holmes asked.

“Why, my brother-in-law and his business associate. But how in blazes did you know?”

“It stands to reason a stranger wouldn’t be allowed into your sanctum, and any employee who left his post without signing in or out would soon be missed. As to where they’ve been lodging, well, one of them – a small man, red-haired, with a fondness for hobnail boots and theatrics – left his trail clear for all to see.”

Hughes’ face turned to a stony glare. “That would be Taverstock. Never met the man myself, tho’ Henry – that’s my brother-in-law – has spoken of him. Local man. Fingers in lots of pies, and, yes, he does have a fondness for what they call amateur dramatics. Crazy for it, apparently. But I won’t believe my own family has been trying to steal from me. George," he said turning to the grizzle-faced man "go fetch Mr. Henry for me. Quickly now."

George, as the elderly engineer proved himself to be, shrugged non-commitally. "He ain't here, that's for sure. Was looking for 'im when I heard all 'ell breaking loose and found these here strays."

We could see that the hatch from which we'd been plucked had been hidden away behind a set of heavy shelves and scuffs on the floor showed that they'd moved many times before this morning.

"These tunnels, George . . . ." Holmes asked.

"Ah! I'd heard tales about the vaults and passages that them diamond cutters were said to have dug, so-as to move stock without being robbed. Regular den of thieves round 'ere. Hatton Gardens being in Cambridge, the City police don't have no jurisdiction, see? Can't be too careful. Never would have believed it, though!"

"Are you saying," Hughes said, slowly, clearly confused, "that Henry and this Taverstock fellow have made off with my plans?"

"Almost certainly. I'd say Henry, having spent some time examining your work and determining which plans were the most valuable, initially tried to have them copied. The doctor's sudden desire to speak to you probably spooked him, so he returned them and decided to bide his time and try again. I'm afraid that our appearance at the Bleeding Heart Tavern yesterday evening may have forced his hand. So he simply stole plans, leaving the way we arrived, meeting Taverstock in the tunnels to make their getaway together. I'd hazard there's a boat moored on the Thames by the sewer outlet at Blackfriars' Bridge."

"Well, good Lord, man! What are we doing standing here? Let's have after them! I'll – "

Holmes held up a hand, cutting Hughes off mid-sentence. "That", he said in a voice, quiet and low, "won't be necessary. See to your sister. She'll need you now."

The weight of Holmes's words seemed to hit Hughes like a brick wall. He reeled, recovered himself somewhat, then nodded soberly. "My God! It's like that, is it? Oh, my poor Edith . . . and the children. Lord, what will I tell them?" He looked at Holmes with a sort of desperation.

"As little as you can. As much as you dare. The police will want to speak to her, but they'll be discrete. I can vouch for that."

"Thank you, Mr. Holmes! I'll go to her right away."

Holmes brushed off any attempts by Hughes to pay for his services and we left the factory in silence, walking once again down Leather Lane towards the small, green, cabman's shelter. There, Holmes turned to me with a look heavy with melancholy.

"Oh, Watson, how I envy you," he said.

"Whatever do you mean?"

"My mind is such that it obsesses over the smallest details. Like a kinesigraph, I see the events of this morning, replay themselves frame-by-frame. I analyze each frame as it flickers past, noting this and that. And do you know which frame sticks most strongly in my mind? The one I see replayed, even now, as we sit in this cab?"

"Why no. What is it?" I asked, alarmed. "Is it something we've missed?"

"No, no. Not at all. It's just a number. A silly, inconsequential number. Six-hundred-and-sixty-six."

"Yes", I whispered, with a rush of that same horror I'd felt earlier. "The number of the beast."

Holmes nodded heavily and tapped the top of the hansom. "221b Baker Street, driver, if you would please. And don't spare the horses."

NOTES

There is indeed a Bleeding Heart Yard and Bleeding Heart Tavern in Hatton Garden.

The cherry tree that the young Elizabeth I is said to have used as a May Pole was in the courtyard of the Mitre Tavern. The tavern is still there and the tree is preserved in the corner of the front bar. It still bloomed until the end of the last century.

The church where Henry VIII and Catherine of Aragon feasted in 1531 is St. Etheldreda's Church. Built in 1291, it is England's oldest Catholic Church, and the only surviving part of Ely Palace, which provided the setting for John of Gaunt's "*This scepter'd isle*" speech in Shakespeare's *Richard II.*

The pieces of poetry that March quotes are from "The House-Warming!!: A Legend of Bleeding-Heart Yard" which appeared in Richard Barham's *The Ingoldsby Legends* (printed in 1837).

In one version of the legend, it is Sir Christopher Hatton's wife who makes a deal with the devil so that Sir Christopher might be a success at Elizabeth's court. In a different account, the victim is Lady Elizabeth Hatton (Sir Christopher's daughter). This version places the murder at Hatton House in 1626, where Elizabeth is murdered by the mysterious Spanish Ambassador, with whom she'd been dancing. When found, her body was torn limb from limb, with her heart still pumping blood onto the cobblestones. Neither of these murders happened but, as Joe says, places don't get called Bleeding Heart Yard for no reason.

Dodson Hughes is undoubtedly Hiram Maxim, inventor of the Maxim machine gun. Presumably Watson changed his name to protect the gentleman's privacy. Maxim had a small factory at 51 Hatton Garden where, in 1881, he started work on his prototype automatic machine gun. In 1891, the British army adopted his invention and it was used to devastating effect during World War I.

Maxim did suffer from bronchitis, and in 1900 began work on the precursor to the modern-day inhaler, which he called his "Pipe of Peace".

Hatton Garden has been the centre of the jewelry trade since medieval times and still boasts a tight-knit Jewish community. Sadly, the kosher cafés, where business was conducted, have all but vanished, as gentrification wipes out another piece of London's distinctive character. The area is believed to have a maze of underground tunnels and vaults. How extensive they are, only the business-owners know.

At the boundary of Clerkenwell and Hatton Garden there's still a manhole cover through which you can hear the sound of the River Fleet, which flows beneath.

The torch that Holmes uses was an 1899 Ever-Ready electric flashlight. Samples were given out to law-enforcement agencies as promotion, which is presumably where Holmes acquired his. The name "flashlight" refers to the fact that they were designed to be used in flashes rather than continuously, which quickly exhausted the battery.

The kinesigraph Holmes references was invented by the wonderfully-named Wordsworth Donisthorpe in 1876. A sequence of prints, mounted on a strip of paper, was rolled on cylinders and passed before the eyes at the same speed as the recording, with electric sparks lighting each print. The only surviving results of his moving picture experiments are ten seconds of a scene in Trafalgar Square, produced around 1889-1890.

The Case of the Impossible Assassin

A man's days are rarely his own – but a married man's are so filled with the pleasures of being friend, husband, provider, and protector, that the past few months had passed in a whirl. Work and home had become the steady metronome of my life, and so settled was I in this new rhythm that I had barely seen my dear friend, Sherlock Holmes. It was, then, with considerable surprise that I opened a telegram to find the following:

> *I travel tonight on the 7 p.m. boat train to Paris. If your wife can spare you for a fortnight, I am in urgent need of my Watson. Bring winter clothing, climbing boots, your revolver, and medical bag. A carriage is reserved.*

Holmes never writes when a telegram will serve and mysterious missives from him were nothing new. I stared at it a while, wondering what strange adventures it might foretell, before passing it across the breakfast table to my wife.

"What do you think?" she asked. "Will you go?"

I shook my head. "Why, my dear, anyone would think that you're tired of me already!"

"Why certainly!" she smiled, delighted at the joke. "How on earth is a woman supposed to get her new home just-so when her new husband is forever under her feet?"

"Well, you did say that you were thinking of inviting your mother to stay to help with the refurbishing. Perhaps I should leave you two to your machinations . . . ." I trailed off laughing.

For a while we sat in silence, until my dearest picked up the telegram again and said, in that thoughtful way of hers, "In earnest, I would not have you abandon your oldest friend in his time of need. Besides, there is still a lot to be done, and I did promise mother a visit once we were settled . . . Perhaps you should take up the offer?"

While I had absolute trust in Dr. Walker to handle the practice in my absence, I was reluctant to abandon my little slice of matrimonial bliss so soon. Hot chocolate was served while we batted the subject back and forth until slowly my reservations abated, and I began to feel that old, familiar thrill stirring in my heart.

Military life had made me a ready traveller and by 6:50 p.m. I was at the station, my old knapsack slung across one shoulder. Holmes had already secured our carriage and, minutes later, I was seated opposite him, exchanging heart-felt greetings.

Slowly, the great glass canopy of Charing Cross Station gave way to rows of sooty terraces and neat urban farms and, soon, we were steaming towards Dover – and adventures yet to come.

It had been a busy time for Holmes with the affair of the Abbey School, the case of poor Lance-Corporal Emsworth, and a commission from the Sultan of Turkey to occupy his finely-tuned mind. And it was of this final, and most mysterious affair, that he now began to speak.

"I must apologize, Watson, for the suddenness of my telegram," he said. "I've been keeping this pot warm for far too long and it has now reached the point where if I do not give it the attention it needs – and in person – the consequences may be catastrophic."

I regarded him – that languid pose, those cool grey eyes with their far-away look – and it seemed inconceivable that one racing towards a case with such weighty consequences could appear so calm. However I knew that, while Holmes could be quite the dramatist, he rarely used hyperbole.

I soon learned that it was to Constantinople we were bound – a journey of sixty-seven hours forty-six minutes from Paris Gare du Nord, according to *Bradshaw's*. London to Dover would take us two hours. Add another one-hour-twenty-five for the Channel crossing. Almost three days! I'd been looking forward to a restful journey, but now I was pleased that I'd thought to pack the back issues of *The British Medical Journal* that I'd been studiously ignoring since my honeymoon!

Holmes stretched out his long legs on the padded bench seat, his own traveling bag stashed behind his head as a makeshift pillow. I was less inclined to use the railway's upholstery in such a cavalier fashion, but made myself as comfortable as I could while Holmes told me what he knew of the case.

"You will no doubt have heard of the First Congress?" he began.

"Republicans, aren't they?" I hazarded, wishing I'd paid more attention to the political pages.

"Ostensibly a collection of liberals fighting for the return of Turkish parliamentary democracy. They held their first meeting in Paris last year."

"Intent on the over-throw of the crown?"

"Hardly. They simply want representation. They have a good-deal of public support too and, on Mycroft's urging, our own government has been discreetly encouraging dialogue between the two parties. Besides, the Sultan is hardly a model ruler."

"Oh? I thought he was considered quite the reformer?"

"He has done much good, but behind the scenes – ? There are rumors. Dark stuff. Mass disappearances. In some quarters he's referred to as 'The Scarlet Sultan' – although I emphasize that these are rumors. Even Mycroft's spiderish network has been unable to discern how much truth there is behind the accusations – and if true – how much the Sultan knows and how much can be laid at the feet of over-zealous panjandrums. One thing is certain: His secret police have too much influence, too little restraint, and the First Congress are in their sights."

"Dangerous?"

Holmes paused, clearly debating exactly how much he could reveal. "This is certainly a delicate situation. We will be working at the behest of the Sultan, and on the recommendation of the British ambassador. That affords us some surety. However, the Sultan's behaviour of late has been irrational. He fears revolution. Mycroft fears that both foreign and Turkish agents are muddying the waters, and manipulating the situation to their own advantage. My brother describes the situation as a primed powder-keg."

"And the *situation*?"

With one of his characteristic bursts of energy, Holmes swung his legs off the seat and bolted upright, his eyes sparkling with that dry glitter which materialized whenever his intellect was challenged.

"Watson!" he said, leaning forwards, his voice a tense whisper. "In all my years investigating the strange and seemingly unfathomable, I have never heard the like! Two of the Sultan's closest advisors – dead – and in circumstances that make the word 'bizarre' seem too commonplace!

"Let me lay it out for you, if I may? I've been so long alone with my thoughts that your clarity and common-sense are much-needed."

I accepted the complement with keen pleasure and I set myself to pay particular attention.

"The commission landed at my door two weeks ago, while I was busy on the Emsworth case. I managed to beg seven day's grace from Dodd to make what plans I could, though I knew I would be unable to travel to Constantinople before today. However, I haven't been idle and here, Watson, we have luck on our side. It seems that detective 'fiction' –" he coughed out the phrase " – is all the rage in Constantinople. Their chief Investigating Officer, Detective Münif, is an ardent fan of your writing and a devoted student of my techniques. I have been provided with the most complete case notes – and every assistance – but clarity still eludes me.

"The victims had been on a hunting trip on the slopes of Mount Kartepe, which lies to the east of Constantinople. The region is mostly thick forest – ancient hazelnut, oak, and chestnut – with one small village perched precariously on the side of the mountain. Locally, the area's known as the Snow

Hills, but the weather this year has been so unpredictable that heavy snowstorms have travelled as far as the metropolis. The men were therefore well-prepared for and – indeed – expecting the worst. But when their bodies were found, they were stark naked!

"Münif has been thorough, meticulously measuring, cataloguing, and recording everything before allowing the bodies to be removed. He has also provided me with photographs of the scene, and the tale these tell is most remarkable.

"Footprints suggest that the victims set off from camp at a veritable sprint, clearly barefooted, but wearing undershirts – cotton fibers were found snagged on the undergrowth. Crushed and broken foliage attests to the fact that they ran desperately, frantically, seemingly without purpose or plan. One of them looks to have fallen down a steep incline, grasping at the earth, pulling up handfuls of frozen grass to slow his descent as he tumbled. Another clearly collided with a tree during his flight – blood on the trunk at head height indicates the severity of the impact. Yet according to locals, the moon was full, and the men knew the terrain well enough to be aware of its dangers.

"Later, the two re-grouped and doubled-back, returning to the tent, one helping support his injured companion. Perhaps they felt the danger had passed and hoped to return to their shelter? If so, they were out of luck. Their tent had been shredded, their supplies burnt.

"It was back at camp, when they should have been safe, that the fatal blow fell. The snow in one spot becomes a riot of confusion – doused in blood. Buffoons in hunting pink would have made a less grisly mess!

"It was there, on the edge of this melee, that their bodies were discovered. Frozen, with bloodied knuckles, bruised skin, and broken teeth suggesting that, in this moment of *extremis*, they had fought for their lives – fought like wild animals – with an enemy that left no tracks behind. No signs at all. And curiouser still was the fact that, in the midst of this life-or-death battle, they found the time to tear off their remaining clothes, for their naked corpses were found lying beside their be-grimed undershirts.

"But, Oh! Watson! What turned the rescue party sick to the stomach wasn't the horror of the scene. No, they were hardened men, fresh from military service. What shocked them were the victim's expressions. Naked terror. That's how and they described it. Pure, naked terror."

"Good Lord!" I exclaimed, horrified. "Wolves? Bears?" I had no idea what wildlife might make its home in these frosty uplands.

"The men had guns. It's unlikely they would have been caught unawares."

"So it's murder, then?"

"It is possible." He paused, lips pursed, as though running through all the permutations of the puzzle. "There are factions upon factions. Anything is possible. Although if murder it is, it's one of the strangest I've ever encountered. The bodies have been kept on ice and I hope, my dear Watson, to employ your expertise here."

"And what if it is the First Congress?"

"Mycroft feels that highly unlikely. They're intellectuals, not revolutionaries, but a pogrom against them would suit many. Foreign agents, as well as those within the country, who fear change. We must tread carefully."

It was not unusual for Holmes to be embroiled in the affairs of state but, suddenly, I felt the weight of his words and my mind reeled.

I believe he was sensitive to the fact, for throughout the rest of the journey, he worked hard to keep me distracted. Holmes could be an entertaining companion when the mood took him and, with my dear friend driving the conversation, my misgivings quickly evaporated.

In a few hours, suburban brick changed to well-hedged fields and soon the cry of seagulls could be heard on the wind. The train pulled up at Dover Harbor and we headed for the promenade dock, embarked on the paddle steamer, and from there onto Paris.

The majestic Gare du Nord is one of the world's busiest and perhaps one of its most beautiful stations. London's great eastern terminus, King's Cross, boasts a glass-roofed train shed nearly seven-hundred-feet long and one-hundred-feet high, but it is still a dark and gloomy beast, seeming to trap in both steam and smoke. Paris' grand station is an altogether airier affair, bathed in natural light from rows of soaring windows, and its own glass and cast-iron roof.

Scottish engineering can take some of the credit for the construction, as its vast girders were made in Glasgow, but French design dominates the whole. It's that, I think, which gives it a lightness of touch and an elegance that's lacking from its British counterparts. In truth, London stations are merely the helpmates of the Empire. Paris' are its galleries.

It was night by the time we arrived in the capital, and the station was illuminated by lanes of gently buzzing electric lights which painted the brickwork a subtle yellow hue. Twenty-three statues stand atop the terminus' triumphal arch, each personifying a different European city. It seemed to me like a stage, set as if for a performance, and I had the odd fancy that the statues were actors, waiting in the wings for their cues.

We took the time to purchase refreshments from one of the many vendors milling around the concourse so that it was close to midnight when we boarded that icon of exoticism: The Orient Express.

I later discovered that the price of a direct ticket between Paris and Constantinople was a quarter of the annual income for the average British worker. Whether our passage had been paid for by Holmes, Mycroft, or the Sultan, I never knew, and never asked, content simply to enjoy such unexpected comfort. Indeed, everything was so well appointed – and the day had been so full of activity – that it wasn't long before I was settled between the freshly-starched sheets and drifting gently off to sleep.

I dreamt of strange things. Tin spinning tops, in the shape of whirling dervishes, with a figure in the shadows pressing the top so that each squealed in distress as they spun. Giant eyes hanging in the sky like over-inflated moons, blinking down at my sleeping form. Then myself suffocating under blankets of snow, with Holmes adding ever more layers until I cried out and woke myself with a start.

Holmes was already awake, savoring a pot of fresh coffee. I helped myself to a cup and, as the world slowly came into focus, I regaled him with the details of my nocturnal adventures.

"Well, Watson," he chuckled, as was his habit when in high spirits, "I don't need to be Sigmund Freud to guess the meaning of such fevered nightmares! I have laid it on rather thickly, haven't I, my dear fellow? Murder and intrigue! Certainly enough to give anyone fever-dreams. Perhaps you'll allow me to stand you breakfast to apologize for my appalling behavior in your dream? Burying you alive indeed!" And with a bark of a laugh, he rang for fresh coffee, as I readied myself to face the day.

From the bright-white tablecloths, to the glittering water decanters, the dining car was everything the well-heeled traveler might expect – but the menu surpassed itself. The galley – squeezed into one end of the dining car – may have been tiny, but the chef's ambition was unbounded. British staples such as haddock, kidneys, kedgeree, porridge, poached egg, and bacon, sat alongside croissant, brioche, freshly-squeezed orange juice, and American dishes such as corn-pone which, despite the unappealing name, turned out to be a type of pancake served with maple syrup.

Having had little food the day before, Holmes and I ate with gusto and sat back to smoke with the blissfully unhurried air of men who, for the time being, had nowhere special to be.

During our long association, I often seen Holmes demonstrate his remarkable observational skills, but this morning his mood was so playful that his pronouncements seemed all the more amazing for the apparent lack of effort he expanded in their making.

“There,” he whispered, sotto voce, “what do you make of him? Sharing the table with the Accidental Heiress and the Jilted Lover?”

I scanned the dining carriage but saw no one fitting those descriptions, which clearly delighted my companion.

“Young lady in bird’s-egg blue with laughing eyes. She sits, stiffly, like someone at church waiting to be denounced for some wrong-doing by the vicar. And see how she fusses at the lace collar and cuffs? They’re too tight, too starched, too new. New pearls as well. A piece of the string from the price tag still clings to the clasp. But that brooch? It’s old, well-worn, very expensive. See, there! She glances around the carriage, notices the elderly lady in the gabardine hat, then looks at the brooch as though recalling the one who gave it to her. Look now, how she half-rises to help waitress with the dishes, then stops herself with a blush. She’s more used to waiting than being waited on, I think. There – her hands. Neatly clipped nails, ruddy knuckles, a little swollen from relentless washing. A nurse or companion to an invalid, I’d vouch, now left a windfall in a will.”

I followed his eye-line to the woman, who did appear woefully uncomfortable among such casual luxury.

“Now . . . there, opposite her. See? The Jilted Lover. Red-rimmed eyes. Dressed without care. See how he continually checks his watch? And in it, a small photograph. See how he smiles and sighs? Even one as unaccustomed to affairs of the heart as I am needs no further clues to tell me this man has a broken heart!

"That leaves the Sallow-Faced Man in the window seat, with the sunken eyes and exorbitant ears. Tell me, what do you make of him?"

I glanced across, scanning for those little clues that Holmes would have found so easily.

"A journalist?" I speculated.

"How so?"

"He's an observer. Interested in what's happening around him, but not partaking. Not a wealthy man, either, which would fit the profession. His cuffs are frayed and – look – the way he counts out the tip. Certainly on a budget. And – yes! As he opened his jacket just then, I saw a notebook. I'd warrant his passage has been paid for by some press agency wanting a piece on the lives of the rich and famous!"

Holmes nodded slowly . "Perfectly sound. But Watson, look again. See the shoes – the soles worn thin. This is a man who does much of his business on foot. See how his eyes dart around the carriage. How he starts at the slightest noise? As you say, he's an observer, but a furtive and highly-strung one. Look how he avoids eye-contact and presses himself into the seat, as though trying to become part of the upholstery. You saw him tipping the waitress, but what you took for penny-pinching was him merely sorting the *francs* from Turkish *lira*.

"Like the young lady, he isn't used to such elegant travel, but he carries an air of authority. Mayhap some of that comes from the small caliber revolver tucked in his pocket. He fingers it almost obsessively, especially whenever he looks in our direction. Or perhaps he carries it for self-defense? I noticed when he entered the carriage that he carries a wound on his shoulder – bullet or knife I cannot tell. Now, remove the whiskers and what have you? Does he remind you of anyone?"

"Why – Lestrade! The man has no physical similarity to the detective we know, but there is something in his bearing that reminds me of the Scotland Yard breed. Yet where Lestrade has loyalty and bull-dog grit, this man seems low and cunning. More than that – I'll vouch he's dangerous."

Holmes fixed his eyes upon me with an amused expression. "That is to be seen. But I think it's safe to say that we've had our first encounter with a member of The Scarlet Sultan's secret police."

Strasbourg, Munich, Vienna, Budapest, and Bucharest all rolled past, and with each arrival and departure, the character of the train shifted. Expressive Mediterraneans were replaced by taciturn Austria-Hungarians and, they, in turn, by neat and formal Asiatics. Hurried businessmen were replaced by wide-eyed tourists, and they in turn, by a more esoteric set. As we drew close to our final destination, it seemed that the whole train now comprised artists, explorers, and spiritualists – a veritable cult of those looking for the un-tangible in the trackless hills of Europe's furthest outpost.

Our meals were enlivened by this constant ebb-and-flow of humanity. Holmes's sharp wit was much employed in its dissection and, notwithstanding our now constant shadow, the journey passed pleasantly.

Constantinople's Sirkeci Station is a place where Europe and Asia collide and its architecture is an appropriate melding of European and Ottoman aesthetics. Swathes of rust-red brick surround wide, arched doorways, and stained-glass windows filter the daylight into colorful splashes of light.

When it opened in 1890, the station was considered a modern marvel. Today, its gas lanterns and Austrian tile stoves already seemed quaint compared to the electrified magnificence of Gare du Nord but, even in the grip of winter, it was warm and inviting. Despite the crowds, everything was well-ordered and clean, with the scent of freshly-ground coffee permeating all.

Detective Münif turned out to be a petite man with a carefully trimmed beard, oiled hair, and a precisely-tailored pinstriped suit. He trotted rather than walked, and if it hadn't been for his facial hair and a certain sharpness about the eyes, I'd have taken him for an over-exited schoolboy playing at detective.

He extended his hand, making a ludicrous half-bow and clicking his heels, German-style. I took his hand, which he pumped up and down enthusiastically, his round face gleaming beatifically. "Mr. Watson! I take the liberty, I know!" he laughed, still pumping furiously. "Such an honor! Such an honor!" He bobbed his head once more then turned his attention to Holmes.

"And the detective himself! Such an honor! Such an honor!"

He babbled on in this vein for some time until Holmes managed to interject. "And when will we be meeting the Sultan?"

"No, no! No one sees the Sultan. However – " And here the little man bent down as if to pick up our bags and whispered in a conspiratorial tone, " – the Sultan sees everyone."

He inclined his head in the direction of the Sallow-Faced Man who had dogged our tracks since Paris, "if you understand my meaning."

We allowed ourselves to be led to a rather preposterous-looking automobile known as a *limousine*. It wasn't until we were settled in its padded interior – the driver safely partitioned from us in his own separate compartment – that Münif stopped his effusive chatter.

"Oh gentlemen! Forgive me! I find the passion of the moment often overcomes good-sense and decorum. I am very honored to have your assistance in this matter. But I believe I may have mentioned that?" He laughed heartily and Holmes shot me the ghost of a smile before addressing himself to the little Turkish detective.

"Our companion on the train, then? The Sallow-Faced Man?"

Münif chuckled appreciatively. "You mean Tekin? As you have no doubt guessed, he's *hafiye*. Police so secret they keep secrets from themselves!"

"It's all a bit much, don't you think?" I said curtly. "We are here on the request on the Sultan, after all!"

"Oh, please do not judge us too harshly" he replied with such good-grace that I immediately regretted my warm words. "Last month there was an attempt on the Sultan's life. It is not widely known but, since the affair, he stays locked in his palace. I have his trust – as do you, gentlemen – but the *hafiye* trust no one. It suits them to keep the Sultan afraid and isolated. Fortunately, humble Münif knows how such games are played!"

Münif's impish manner was tempered with a quiet self-confidence that quickly won us over. The car sped onwards and upwards. The driver attacked the narrow mountain roads with an alarming lack of concern for either the wildlife or the nerves of his passengers, so that it was with some relief that we finally we reached the tiny hamlet clinging to slopes of Snow Hill.

After a simple but hearty meal in the village café, we were led to a roughly-hewn chapel which had been converted into a make-shift morgue – its windows left ajar to keep the bodies chilled.

It was a singular place of blasted stonework and arrow-slit windows that seemed more pagan than Christian in these primordial wilds. Its quietness and remoteness were both calming and unnerving.

The bodies lay upon the bare altar table, their injuries all the more hideous for the alabaster paleness of their dead flesh. Their faces were indeed a vision of terror. Even in death they were horribly contorted and their glassily staring eyes and bared teeth produced such a sinister impression upon my mind that it left me momentarily speechless.

Holmes was not unaffected. His black brows drew down, his forehead contracted, and he stood absorbed in thought for many minutes. When he spoke in was in a tone of hushed reverie.

"The word '*mortuary*'," he began, "has its roots in the Latin '*mortuus*', meaning '*death*'. The French '*morgue*' has an altogether stranger meaning: '*To look at solemnly; to defy*'. Even for one such as myself, who has seen much death, the solemnity of an occasion such as this never leaves me. But '*defy*' is an odd word in this context, don't you think, Watson? Defy: '*To challenge, to resist, to be strange or extreme*'. Life is, perhaps, a constant challenge to death. Every morning that we wake and greet a new day, we resist Death's icy fingers. But is death strange or extreme? I would say no. It is perfectly mundane. A cause and effect. We live – therefore we must die. But here we have death both strange *and* extreme."

I had felt uneasy since that first night aboard the Orient Express, and Holmes's words chilled me such that I went about the little room lighting lanterns, like a child trying to throw off their night-fears.

Finally, when I had steadied myself sufficiently, we began the autopsy.

Münif had provided everything necessary, but informed us that the deceased must remain anonymous, for fear that news of their untimely deaths would precipitate some great crisis. So it was that we began work on two men who we knew only as "*Grey Hair*" and "*White Beard*".

The men were in their forties, stockily built, with muscular inner thighs and glutes, and several enthesophytes – those bony projections that appear at the attachment point of tendons or ligaments, caused by repeated stress. Both of these were suggestive of a lifetime spent in the saddle. Various external wounds, long healed, identified them as military men – so likely cavalry rather than wealthy horse-fanciers.

Holmes's knowledge of pathology was first-rate and, combined with my more practical experience, the chain of events began to reveal themselves.

White Beard had defensive cuts and bruises – imprints of Grey Hair's knuckles were clearly visible on his face. Traces of Grey Hair's skin, found under White Beard's nails, confirmed the truth. Rather than being assailed by a third party, the one man had seemingly attacked the other. The cause of such startling behaviour was soon made clear.

The cheeks, chin, and nose of both victims were mottled, and a purple rash lay over the large joints of the extremities, which was easily distinguished from the normal *livor mortis* seen in dependent areas of the body.

Despite their bloody appearance, none of the wounds were fatal, nor were traces of toxins to be found. Experience had taught me that, often, the more mysterious a puzzle seems, the more mundane the solution, and this appeared to be the case. These men had died of hypothermia, in which extreme instances a person becomes disoriented, confused, and combative. Finally, as vasoconstriction fails, warm blood flows back into the frozen skin, producing a false feeling of extreme warmth. This sensation of burning heat causes the dying man to throw off his clothes – sealing his fate.

We worked together, for the most part in silence, each confident in the other's skills, until finally Holmes exclaimed, "No, no! There are still too many questions!"

"But it is not murder," I replied. "No third party need be tracked and punished. Surely that will serve?"

"No, Watson!" He said with a flash of red-hot energy. "It simply will not do! Let us start at the beginning, not at the end. What drove them to this point? Why did two men leave their tents in the middle of the night, in such a hurry, that they did not bother to arm themselves or dress? Surely the danger must have been great indeed, to put military men in such fear for their lives that they gave no thought to fighting, hiding, or running for aid? Instead they propelled themselves off cliff edges and into trees. And what danger is it that comes in the night and leaves no trace? No, this mystery deepens by the moment."

Holmes's words struck home. Whatever the truth, the dead had told us all they could.

Münif was eager to hear our findings, regarding Holmes with a quiet reverence as my companion outlined our progress.

When he was finished, Münif nodded thoughtfully. Despite the grim nature of the discussion, his face was a picture of unfettered delight, but his eyes told a more interesting tale. I was beginning to suspect that "humble Münif" was not altogether what he appeared.

"Interesting, very interesting!" he said. "You will want to stay a night or two at the victim's camp?"

"Quite so," Holmes replied.

Münif clapped his hands. "I had anticipated such a request!"

"Will you join us?" I asked.

"It has been my dearest wish! But, now, come, you must be weary. There's a room above the café which has been secured for you. Call for Baris should you need anything."

I awoke early the next morning. The previous day's adventures had given me another restless night and I was filled with strange forebodings.

Holmes was already awake and it seemed to have been for many hours. He sat on the small bed, cross-legged like some Eastern mystic, his old briar thrust out as a challenge to the day. The coverlet was thrown back and strewn with papers – the bottom sheet covered in pencilled notes!

The air was heavy with tobacco and I crossed to the window to let in a little air. It was as I reached for the casement lock that I glanced down and my heart turned to lead. Sallow-Face!

"Ah" Holmes said languidly. "You've noticed our visitor?"

"Lord! How long has he been here?"

"He's been haunting the courtyard all night. For a secret policeman, he's abominably heavy footed."

"What? Have you been awake all night then?"

"I have, and it has been most instructive. Yet, as to the case . . . I have turned it over and over in my mind and found no explanation that appears adequate."

He gestured vaguely to the papers on the bed. "Everything I have – topographical maps, Münif's notes and photographs. But I don't like it! Everything screams that a crime has been committed. That men were driven into the snow to die. How? Who is this impossible assassin? Where is the evidence?" For a moment his eyes fixed vacantly upon the frost-tinted window then he leapt to his feet with a sudden exclamation. "Come! Daylight is wasting."

I rapidly threw on my clothes and navigated the winding, unlit staircase to find Münif – red faced and panting – already in conference with Holmes in the café below.

"It seems, my dear Watson, that Münif has also spotted our clod-footed shadow and has just been in pursuit of the fellow."

“Alas!” the detective said. “He fled. Vanished into trees, like the sneaking wolf he is.”

“Should we be worried?” I asked.

For a moment Münif did indeed look worried. Then his round face lit up and he said, with a toothy smile. “Ah, what concern is one plodding *hafiye* when the Baker’s Road Men are on the scent!”

It was hard not to find the little man’s energetic speech amusing, but when I glanced at Holmes I noted that he looked at the colorful fellow with an icy detachment. What it meant I couldn’t discern, for the detective kept us quite occupied for the next hour, as breakfast was served and he outlined the journey we would be making.

I was pleased to discover that the Turks took breakfast as seriously as the British. Doughy, sesame-seed-coated bread, soft goat’s cheese, succulent olives, rich molasses, a fragrant bergamot jam, eggs, and spicy beef sausage made a tasty spread. By the time we had eaten, the early morning chill had abated and we were full of fuel for the day’s exertions.

The morning was icy-blue and locked in frost. There wasn’t a cloud in the sky, and our breath blew out such plumes of smoke that we seemed to be miniature steam engines. The snow lay thick and deep, allowing the use of skis, although the wooded nature of the terrain meant that we must walk with them, Nordic style.

Münif declared that he hadn’t seen such weather since he was a child, though he moved through the drifts with an enviable nimbleness.

It wasn't long before I began to fall behind the company, and I was grateful when Holmes slowed his pace to join me.

"Watson," he hissed as I came within ear-shot, "no time to explain, but be on the alert. This is a singular and a dangerous web we have become embroiled in – "

Münif appeared at Holmes's heels like an over-eager puppy. My friend fell instantly silent, leaving my mind to grapple with the significance.

We climbed into the clouds for many hours. The sun shone brightly, at times reflecting off the snow to such effect that I was dazzled. By afternoon, the chill had begun to creep into my boots and beneath my heavy Norfolk. My pack got weightier, and my legs heavier, so that by the time we finally reached the location of the crime, I felt quite spent.

There was little left to indicate the tragedy that had occurred. Weeks of snow had covered what remained of the camp, but that didn't stop Holmes's keen eyes from surveying the scene.

Münif busied himself building a small fire and soon tin mugs of steaming coffee were handed round to all. It was a local blend, bitter in taste, which Münif explained was best taken sweetened with molasses. Holmes seemed to relish the brew and drank one cup after another. I drank it for the warmth it brought but, rather than revive me, I found that it increased my lethargy to the point where I could barely keep my eyes open.

It was then that I glanced at Holmes, who sat furiously blinking, cup discarded at his side, the thick treacly liquid forming a rivulet in the snow. His face was pale and a glitter of moisture sat on his brow. I saw his head fall, dragging his tall form backwards into the snow. A low, buzzing alarm began to sound somewhere in my mind. Vague shapes swirled and swam in warning of some unknowable horror. A sinking fear took possession of me – but it was too late! I heard myself cry out. Then I too followed Holmes into the deep and dreamless sleep that laudanum brings.

What happened next only Holmes can tell, and I report his words as accurately as I can.

"I know well," he began "the taste of laudanum and a few gulps of Münif's coffee told me that the drink had been heavily laced with the drug. I had drunk enough – and quickly – to feel its effects and did, in truth, succumb for some time.

"I awoke to find the little Turk shredding our packs, disposing, I assumed, of anything that might give us shelter or warmth, for it seemed clear that he intended to leave us at the mercy of the elements.

"I lay there, limbs slowly succumbing to the cold, determined to play dead until I could get the upper hand, when suddenly the wind began to rise. With it came a curious noise. I am not, I think, easily unnerved, but there was something about that low keening that stopped the blood in my veins. It continued for some time, creating a sensation of intense pressure about the head. I had the ridiculous impression that something was actually inside my skull trying to claw its way out. At the same time, I felt all control of my body slipping away. My limbs began to twitch, my vision blurred, and soon I could taste my own blood which was flowing so freely from my nose that I was beginning to choke on it. I knew with absolute certainty that if I did not flee from that spot in the instant, I would be a dead man.

"And flee I did, insensible to my surroundings, aware only of the growing terror that the Siren's song brought. I ran like a man possessed, howling, tearing at my hair, limbs thrashing out at foliage which, in my fever, I imagined to be assailants. At times I ran like Alice's Red Queen, seemingly going nowhere. At others, I found myself on familiar London streets, being pursued by I know not who. At one point I saw Münif – though I saw so many things which could not be accounted real, that he too may have been a phantom of the mind. He ran like the very devil was on his heels, quite outpacing me, his face a picture of madness. In such confusion as I found myself, I would have run straight off the hill-side had not our trustworthy shadow brought me down with doughty rugby tackle."

While Holmes raged and howled on that unforgiving mountain, I slept the sleep of the dead. How long I remained unconscious I couldn't tell. It must have many hours, for when I awoke the moon had already risen. I was chilled, heavy headed, and utterly alone!

Once again the camp was a scene of mayhem – our meagre packs scattered. I saw signs of chaos, of panic, and footprints leading down the hill, which I dared not follow.

My body was weary and stiff, yet my mind was at the highest pitch of tension so that every sound, every motion set my nerves on edge. I sat thus for many hours, half-inclined to head out in search of Holmes, half-afraid that should I move, Holmes would return and miss me in the darkness. Logic told me to stay put, so I did what I could to make a beacon for my friend, setting a fire from lichen and strips of my tattered pack which lit up the mountainside like the flare from a Very gun.

I had just begun to despair when two figures emerged from the tree-line. Never have I seen a more welcome sight: Holmes! And supporting his gaunt figure – not the little Turkish detective, but Sallow-Face himself.

There was no time to wonder what this could mean. I jumped up and, between us, we helped Holmes to the fire. His face was drawn, much bloodied, bruised, and covered in a dozen cuts, but otherwise he seemed unharmed.

It didn't take long for the fire and a tot or two of whisky from my flask to do the trick.

"Watson," he said with more vigor than I could credit, "may I introduce the *real* Detective Münif."

I sat blinking stupidly for some time. "Well, who then was Münif?"

"Why," Holmes coughed out a hollow chuckle, "the *real* Tekin!"

"What? How long have you known?"

"I have suspected *something* for a while. It seemed strange to me that a humble detective should know the identities of the Sultan's most secret police by name. Then there were other smaller things. He called you 'mister', not 'doctor'. He spoke of '*Baker's Road*', not '*Baker Street*'. Regardless of the eccentricities of speech, it seemed unlikely that the real Münif – who was such an admirer – would make such mistakes. To my mind, there seemed something too studied, too dissembling about the character he presented to us. But I didn't have anything to support my suspicions until I spoke to the detective, here, last night."

Not for the first time in our long association I felt at a loss. "Why the deception?"

"I believe he saw in our arrival an opportunity. Already two men close to the Sultan were dead. Should we, too, be found dead – think of the ramifications. Think who could be blamed and fitted for the crime. Remember – Mycroft warned us that the *hafiye* had the First Congress in their sights? If the false Münif spoke one true thing during our association I'd wager it was this: '*It suits the* hafiye *to keep the Sultan afraid and isolated*'."

"Did he not imagine the real Münif would arrive to unmask him?"

Our shadow had said little up to this point, but when he spoke it was in the thankfully sober and plain tones of a policeman – quite the contrast to his impersonator! "That would have been difficult, Doctor, for you see, I am dead. Or so he believed. His assassin's bullet very nearly did its job. It was then that I decided to 'lay-low', as the detective novels term it. I am sorry if my appearance on the train unnerved you. If he wanted me out of the way, then it seemed reasonable to assume that he wanted you out of the way too. So I played guard-dog and waited to see what would transpire."

"This is incredible!" I said. "But – wait! We're still no further on. We still don't know what it was that drove Grey Beard and White Hair almost mad with fear."

"And me as well," Holmes added. He sat wrapped in the tattered remains of our camp blankets, a fresh pipe glowing, looking for all the world like he was reclining in his chair at

Baker Street rather than perched in alien snowscape. "Now that I've had time to think on it, I'll tell you what I believe. Much is beyond proof.

"You'll remember, perhaps, Tesla's earthquake machine, which nearly caused the death of the great Mark Twain some years back? The device was found to dangerously aggravate anyone who came within close proximity. The low vibrations it created were much like those that make sand dunes appear to sing. The same thing happens when winds rush down elevated slopes at great speeds. I had heard it said in Switzerland that such singing was able to drive a man mad. I think," Holmes continued, rubbing his bruises ruefully, "that we now have good reason to believe the veracity of such tales!"

My friend had once said, "Eliminate the impossible and whatever remains, no matter how improbable, must be the truth – " But what a truth! As we sat, allowing the fire to warm our bones, my mind turned to tales of Homer. To sailors driven to self-destruction by songs carried on the wind. And I marveled at the strangeness of a world that seemingly had such things in it.

Soon the sun had risen, and our little party gathered what kit we could for the journey back to the village. Our progress was a slow but, despite events, I felt lighter than I had for days.

Detective Münif – the *real* Münif – had every confidence that with Tekin dead, the *hafiye* would not dare dispute his account of events. Indeed, everything was tied up so swiftly and neatly that by the next evening we were back at Sirkeci Station, boarding the Orient Express for London.

As we sat that night in the dining car, watching Istanbul slowly disappear from view, Holmes drew my attention to the table opposite. There were the Accidental Heiress and the Jilted Lover, hands clasped across the table in an attitude of complete devotion.

Holmes, naturally, affected his usual half-cynical vein, but to see how this romance had blossomed quickly set me thinking on my own good fortune.

As Holmes had noted, Dr. Freud would have had no difficulties diagnosing the cause of the strange forebodings that had dogged me since this case began. Part of me, I think, had been afraid that I might lose what I had only just won. Yet in three days, I would be back in the arms of dearest wife and, at the thought, I couldn't help but smile and quietly wish this new couple as much happiness as I had found.

NOTES

In the 1900s, Istanbul was indeed crazy for detective fiction. The sultan himself was a huge aficionado.

Sand dunes do sing. When Marco Polo first heard it in China, he ascribed the sounds to evil spirits. Similar 'songs' have also been reported on steep mountains.

Tesla's earthquake machine was bizarrely used in 1890 to help his friend, Mark Twain, who was constipated. It's reported that the effects were so dramatic Tesla feared for his friend's life.

Natural or man-made ultra- low frequency sounds (under 10Hz) can cause mental and physical distress when they're powerful enough – and played for long enough. Military experiments with ultra-low frequencies, as part of psy-op operations, reported exposure to such sounds could induce fear, vertigo, disorientation, visual distortions, and heart attacks. In nature katabatibc winds, which form on steep mountains, may generate similar ultra-low frequency vibrations and have been suggested as the cause several mysterious hiking accidents.

The Adventure of the Cable Street Mummy

I had not long been resident in Baker Street and was still learning to accommodate myself to the peculiar customs of a fellow lodger who imagined that a jack-knife plunged into the heart of an elegant, Georgian fireplace was a fine place to keep his correspondence.

I nevertheless considered myself fortunate to have landed so firmly on my feet in this great wilderness of a city, for I doubt that I will ever again find such well-appointed rooms or such a fascinating and agreeable companion as Sherlock Holmes.

While his moods could be extreme, and his habits trying, it was the very contradictions in his nature that I found so compelling. He could be thoughtless, but was never mean-spirited. His studies were well-ordered and methodical, but he was a bohemian at heart. He affected a detached coolness towards the world, but exalted in music and good food. And, while he professed to care neither for society nor company, I had quickly come to regard him as a loyal and true friend.

I had risen early – a practice formed in the long days of student study and forged into habit chasing Ghazi coat-tails through Afghanistan. Holmes had hurried off the previous evening on some mysterious mission and not yet returned. So it was that I found myself a watcher at the window, and quickly fell into a brown study, musing on the press and swell of London life – still so new to me.

Our diggings lie but three minutes from Baker Street East underground station, with Regent's Park to the north and Mayfair to the south. It's a handsome house, brick-built with – or so our redoubtable landlady, Mrs. Hudson, tells me – six bedchambers, three sitting-rooms and, in the basement, a kitchen, scullery, housekeeper's room, butler's pantry, China closet, and larder. Upon inheriting the freehold from her deceased husband, Mrs. Hudson had divided up the property and I found myself in the agreeable position of going halves on rooms that I would never have been able to afford with my own depleted finances.

Mrs. Hudson had once commented that "a property is a nice thing to have but an expensive thing to maintain", yet it appeared to me she cared less for financial gain than the pleasure of being a landlady. There was an element of proprietorial pride in that slow, dignified tread of hers – like a head of state inspecting her troops.

She had just laid the breakfast table and was turning to leave with the same unhurried air. I nodded my thanks and made a bee-line for the coffee pot.

A pall of early morning chimney smoke filled the sky, and the day appeared to have settled into a resigned, uniform grayness. "My, but it's a gloomy day" she sighed.

"It is, indeed, Mrs. Hudson," I replied. "Does it never make you long for home? The open skies of the Highlands?"

"Oh, rarely" she said. "As I grow older, I find I've an independent streak that does not sit well with my Presbyterian kin. No, London suits me very well and lets me suit myself. Besides," she added, waving a hand at the unruly piles of books, clippings, file-boxes, retorts, test-tubes, and little Bunsen lamps scattered around the sitting room "who else would put up with their home being so cruelly abused?"

"Ah, well, you should perhaps retire before I empty the contents of this bag onto that very welcome breakfast table," Holmes announced from the doorway, with a gleeful laugh.

The landlady turned, tutted and, eyeing Holmes with the look of a woman indulging a recalicant child, quickly retreated.

"Give me a hand Watson, I don't think Mrs. Hudson would thank me if I ruined her best table cloth."

I moved the breakfast things over to the side-table and watched Holmes pull a piece of oilcloth from the voluminous pockets of his overcoat. He rolled out the cloth and placed – rather gingerly, it seemed to me – a doctors' bag on top. It was of the common design but I noted, enviously, that while mine still had the scent and sheen of new leather, his was a venerable thing, covered in all manner of chemical burns and greasy stains.

He opened the brass clasp with a snap and, with the attitude of a magician pulling a rabbit out of a hat, produced an object roughly the size of an human head wrapped in a sac, tied with string. With a flourish, he pulled the cord that kept the cloth fastened and the sac's contents tumbled onto the oil cloth.

Dear Lord! It was a head! And what a thing! Blackened skin and clumps of matted hair still clung to the skull. Its eyes, surrounded by sunken hollows, were open, so that it seemed to regard one with a steady yet horribly vacant gaze. Its mouth was agog, its tongue emerging from an avenue of splintered teeth like a bloated slug. “Good grief!” I gagged “Where on Earth did you get such a thing?”

“At the crossroads of Cable Street and Cannon Street where, in keeping with tradition, its owner had been buried, head first, with a stake through his heart.”

“You can’t be serious? I spluttered. “But who is it?”

“Watson,” Holmes replied with an amused smile, “meet Able Abless.”

I blinked stupidly and Holmes returned my blank stare, looking rather deflated.

“The name means nothing to you, then?”

“Should it?”

“Ah, Watson, you’re no student of crime. Forty years ago Able here,” he said patting the thing affectionately,” was probably one of the most famous men in the empire.”

Now, I’m a medical man, and have seen things that would make the strongest stomach protest, but for some reason this curious mummy and Holmes's evident glee at its acquisition quite turned my veins to ice. “For heavens sake put the poor fellow back in the bag and tell me what this is all about!”

“Oh, my dear Doctor forgive me!” Holmes said, sounding quite chastised. “I sometimes forget myself. You’re right, of course. The breakfast table is no place for the head of one of London’s most notorious murderers. Now, draw up a chair and, while I’m no storyteller, I guarantee that what I’m about to relate will make this grisly interlude well worth your while.”

I claimed myself a cup of thick, black coffee and settled myself in the basket-chair. Holmes took the easy-chair and assumed his usual position, his long, thin legs stretched out towards the fire. Eyes closed, fingers steepled, he began.

"On Saturday 5th November, 1842, at around eleven p.m., Bartholomew Jameson, the owner of a tailor's shop at number 25 Pennington Street was preparing to close his business for the night. Saturday was then the usual day for workers to be paid, and being so near Christmas, businesses opened early and closed late. His wife was nursing their newborn son, so he sent out their serving girl, Maggie, for oysters as a treat, while he and his assistant closed up shop. This was to be the last time Maggie would see any of them alive again.

"Even in the gloom, winding her way through the close-pressed streets, the errand should have taken no more than twenty minutes. But, tonight, she was out of luck. Or maybe in luck, considering what was about to happen.

"It was a chill evening. A river mist was beginning to creep up the lanes, blanketing the houses, so that she had to stop several times to ensure she hadn't missed her turning. To make matters worse, every shop she tried was shuttered. Determined to find some oysters for her young mistress, she pressed on towards the High Street – a leery place at that time of night, with the Thames-side inns still doing lively business. It had gone midnight and she was beginning to despair of ever completing her errand when she literally stumbled into a street-seller, weaving home with his barrow, who was happy to let the last of his oysters go for a penny.

"Rushing back, Maggie clearly heard the bells of St. George's ringing the quarter hour. Increasingly anxious, worried she'd be in trouble for taking so long, she picked up the pace. Trotting the rest of the way – heeled boots on cobbles telegraphing her progress – she arrived at Pennington Street, red-faced and breathing hard.

"The shop was in darkness. She pulled the bell, but got no reply. She rang over and over. Still nothing. After almost ten minutes, she was feeling so sorely used, she began to kick the door, believing that the family had forgotten about her and left her out in the cold.

"It was a single sound that changed her growing frustration to fear. A scream – high and piercing'.

"Once again the girl hoisted up her skirts and ran pell-mell towards the river where she managed to persuade a young officer of the River Police to return with her to the house. They arrived to discover the neighbor, who owned the pawnbrokers next door, hammering on the door. He claimed to have been awoken by a loud thump 'as though something wet was being thrown against the adjoining wall', followed by an anguished cry, cut off by what he described as a 'terrible gurgle, like someone drowning'.

"The officer, Peter Hore, made for the rear of the block of terraces and, finding the gate locked, scaled the high wall that enclosed the family's small back yard. Nothing, I think, could have prepared him for the scene that he found there. The smell reached him first – a tang of copper and human excrement: The scent of death.

"The back door was open, and in the feeble light of his lantern, he saw what he at first took to be a bag of coal. It was only as he moved closer that the flickering torch revealed the gory truth. The body of Bartholomew Jameson, lying in a corridor painted red with his own blood. His head, or what remained of it, had been reduced to little more than a sack of pulp and bone shards. The young assistant lay beside his master, the lower half of his face missing. His neck broken with such force that the coroner would note that several of the cervical vertebrae had been reduced to dust. A shipwright's maul, which seemed to have inflicted such terrible violence, was found at the foot of the stairs.

"Officer Hore later speculated that the master and his assistant had died first, and the assailant had dropped the maul as he was making for first floor bedroom. Not an unreasonable assumption and, as it turns out, entirely correct.

"It was in those upper chambers, that perhaps the most pitiful scene was to be found. The young mother lay by the crib, a carpenter's chisel forced with such violence into her neck that it had pinned her to the floor boards. The body of the young boy, still wrapped in his swaddling clothes, was found close by. On the wall was a scarlet smear where the child had been hurled against the brick – accounting for the strange damp thud heard by the neighbor.

"As shocking as these events were, however, this was just the beginning of the evening's horrors. While Officer Hore was busy searching the scene, a few streets away, a second, equally monstrous, equally senseless attack was taking place. This time, there was a witness.

"Ichabod Monmouth had lived at Number 17 Waterman Way for two years. He rented a modest room from his employer, Samuel Black, for whom he worked as an arkwright, making sea chests for the sailors in nearby Tobacco Dock. At 10.30 p.m., Saturday, being his half-day, he returned from a convivial night in The Painted Stag, made small talk with Mr. and Mrs. Black, then retired to bed. He was awoken two hours later by the sounds of, as he put it, 'bloody murder being done'. Opening his bedroom door, he was confronted by the shadowy outline of two figures. The intruders were evidently too intent on their work to notice they were being observed. One was slight of frame with a perceptible limp. The other he described as 'a square, mountainous brute'.

"Although he'd later be branded a coward, it's clear from his account that Monmouth exhibited remarkable presence of mind. Knowing he couldn't tackle the intruders alone, he quietly closed his bedroom door, and using his sheets as a rope, clambered from his window and – barefoot, in his nightshirt – ran for help.

"By the time the police arrived, the murderers had bolted, leaving behind a trail of gory bootprints and three mangled bodies. There was also one tangible clue that was filed away as evidence and never referred to again – a hand-print left on the apprentice's nightshirt by the cut and still bleeding hand of his murderer."

For a while, Holmes sat in silence. I knew from his drawn brows and keen face that his mind was busy, as was mine, in picturing those tragic events. Finally, it was I who broke the silence.

"And this is the man who committed these atrocities?" I asked, looking across at the doctor's bag with a renewed and, admittedly, somewhat morbid interest.

"He was certainly arrested for the deeds but no one – not even, I fear, the authorities – truly believed he was guilty. The evidence was flimsy to say the least. Our only witness, Monmouth, described two assailants, and Abless fitted neither description. And, while he was known to the first victim, he had no connection to the second. A shipwright's maul, which was supposed to have the initials *A.A.* carved into its handle, miraculously materialized some time after his arrest. The original case notes make no mention of a such detail, nor do contemporary illustrations show any inscriptions on the murder weapon."

"But, then why – ?"

"Conjure, if you will, the scene. Seven brutal deaths. Two women. One child. Innocents. A close-knit community. Emotions running hot. So hot, that the police feared a riot. The Magistrate at the time wrote '*I am vexed with myself ... my desire for discovering the atrocious murderers may have run me into error.... I fear my zeal has not been within proper bounds.*' Note he said '*murderers*'.

"So you think it was what our American friends would call 'a frame-up?'"

"I have long suspected so but, as of some months ago, I can confidently say that I now know Able Abless was completely innocent."

"Yet he was still hanged?"

"Not at all. I believe he was murdered before his name could be cleared. The authorities claimed he had taken his own life, which explains why he was buried in such a bizarre manner. Suicides are prone to spectral wanderings – or so I hear" Holmes added with a ghoulish grin.

I was lost and admitted as much. "Now, look Holmes, I agree that all this makes for a spectacularly grotesque breakfast. But you say you can now *prove* that he was innocent. How? And how the deuce do you come to have his head?"

"I said I knew that he was innocent. Proof is something else entirely. But, courtesy of the gentlemen who unearthed Mr. Abless for me yesterday evening, that's exactly what I hope to be able to do. Now," Holmes sprang up with one of his characteristic bursts of energy, "if you're free, I would be very pleased if you could accompany me to Wapping. I'd like to introduce you to the rest of poor Able." And that was all he could be compelled to say until we alighted at the church St. George in the East, where a little mortuary stood, looking sadly forlorn in the shadow of Hawksmoor's grand Baroque church.

Able Abless had died and been buried ten years before I was born. He had been interred without coffin or shroud and his corpse seeded with quicklime. After forty years lying in thick mud, there should have been very little left of him beyond softened bones. The fact that he was in such a remarkable state of preservation was, according to Holmes, due to a combination of waterlogged London clay, a succession of cold winters, and the quicklime itself, which destroyed the very bacteria that, ordinarily, would have made a feast of Abless' sorry remains.

I have noted previously the eccentric nature of Holmes's knowledge and it now appeared that I was to add "a disturbing understanding of the decomposition process" to the plus side of his tally. "I've been testing pig corpses under a variety of conditions," was his alarming admission. "Rather than aid decomposition, quicklime appears to act as a preservative," he noted, his dark eyes sparking. I made a mental note not to follow up on that particular conversation!

I was already acquainted with his uncannily preserved head, but Abless' body, was even more of a surprise. His skin, though as tanned as leather and lying on his bones like a deflated hydrogen balloon, was soft and moist. His muscles still allowed for the arms and legs to flex at the joints. I could see that an autopsy had been recently completed and Holmes confirmed that the organs and blood vessels were also intact. More amazing was that there was still liquid blood in his veins. It was all so uncanny, that I found myself imagining that the cloying London clay in which Abless had been lying had seeped into his body, replacing flesh and bone with some golum-esque simulacrum – and I shuddered at the thought of it.

"I have long held that science lies at the heart of detection," Holmes commented, in a tone of barely suppressed excitement. "It may, one day, be possible to look at a body such as this and know the entirety of its history with absolute certainty … ." He paused a moment, looking wistful for, as I imagined it, some far-future discoveries, then, continued, "No matter. Mr. Abless may keep his secrets for now but he can still be of assistance. In this instance, I believe comparative dactylography may offer some intriguing possibilities."

"Finger … *graph*?" I hazarded, my Greek not being what it should be.

"Exactly so. As you are no doubt aware, the front or palmar surface of the hands are marked with *rugae* – folds and ridges. Dr. Faulds' article in *Nature,* 'On the Skin-Furrows of the Hand', contended that the scroll-like patterns found on the finger-tips display infinite variety, and he even outlined a technique for their capture. As a mater of interest, he postulated that this technique could be used both on mummies and bloody finger-marks left on objects where crimes have occurred," Holmes added with an amused bark.

"Well, we certainly have a mummy. But do we have any bloody finger-marks?" I asked, fairly certain what Holmes's response would be.

For a reply, he hauled a large basket from beneath the work bench which contained, amongst other curious items, what was quickly identified as a soiled nightshirt. "We do, thanks to the foresight of Officer Hore and the archives of Thames River Police. We're lucky this was such a high-profile case. But who do they belong to, hmmm? That's the question."

Holmes plundered the basket once more and pulled out a piece of slate, a bottle of black, lithographic ink, a small printer's roller, a sea-sponge, some sheets of paper, and – most curious of all – a magic lantern and a collection of glass slides to use within.

"Now, Watson, if you could moisten this sponge, and use it to dampen one of these sheets of paper, I'd very obliged. Damp, mind, not wet."

I did as requested while Holmes splashed some of the pungent, viscous ink onto the slate, using the roller to spread it evenly over the surface. "Now, we shall see!" he exclaimed.

I watched, spellbound for a moment, as Holmes manipulated Abless' corpse – all the more terrible for its unnatural suppleness. He rolled the right thumb onto the inked slate then, motioning me to hand him the paper, transferred the sticky print to the sheet. He strode over to the bench once more and pressed the paper onto one of the glass slides.

He then took out his watch and, as he counted off the seconds, I saw his apprehension grow. I had come to recognize a thousand tiny signs which reflected the great emotions that assaulted him in moments such as this: When he pitted his titanic intellect against the world.

As the minute-hand completed its sweep, Holmes, with a remarkable delicateness of touch, peeled the paper from the glass. Success!

"Ha! Ha!" he cried, clapping his hands in a paroxysm of excitement. "Magnificent! Just magnificent! A little faint, but it will do, Watson! It will do! Now come here, and we'll see what we shall see."

I edged around the autopsy table, crammed, as it was, into the woefully small work space, to stand beside him. He lit a candle and closed the mortuary's heavy shutters. Then, popping the candle into the space behind the projector, he angled the magic lantern towards the blank wall. "Look, now. Here is a slide I prepared from a photograph of the blooded thumb left on the poor victim's nightshirt. And here – " He placed the slide he had just prepared in the slot behind, so that the two images were superimposed one upon the other – "is the imprint of Abless' thumb. You'll agree that, even with the difficulties involved in getting a clear image from the cloth, there's no possibility of these belonging to the same man?"

I admitted as much.

"And now?" He removed the new slide and replaced it with another from the pile. Heavens! It was a match! "But where did you get this imprint? I asked – not for the first time in my dealings with Holmes – feeling a little lost.

Holmes raised his hand. "I promise you Watson, that within the hour you'll know everything I do, but for now allow me to indulge my sense of dramatic by admitting that I have an unfair advantage. I know something that only one other living person knows."

Back at Baker Street we were informed by Mrs. Hudson that there was a caller awaiting our return.

I recognized the white-haired gentleman from his previous visits and had already extended my hand in welcome as Holmes began to make the formal introductions. So, it was that I found myself in the uncomfortable position of shaking the hand of a man I'd much rather have knocked to the ground.

"Watson," Holmes said, "I'd like you to meet David Mathers, who the press so luridly dubbed at the time, 'The Shadwell Slaughterer'."

I recoiled, as though bitten by a cobra, and shot Holmes a look of protest.

"Please, Watson, do sit down and allow Mr. Mathers the curtesy of telling you his story in his own words."

I confess I did not like the way that everything, from the morning's exposition over the breakfast table to Mathers' appearance in our rooms, seemed to have been orchestrated. Not did I care to be told to extend the social niceties to a murderer. But I did as Holmes requested, while our guest paced the floor and related one of the most ghastly tales it's been my misfortune to hear.

Despite his white-hair, Mathers was still a vigorous-looking man – large, square of shoulders, with the sort of ruddy complexion that comes from years of drink and manual labour. "I didn't come 'ere to ask for forgiveness for what I done," he began, casting me a look that seemed to suggest otherwise. "I've been to the police and got nowhere. Not that I blame them. I ain't got no proof of what I say. That's why I came to Mr. Holmes. A fine turnabout when a criminal needs a private copper to help prove his guilt – and no mistake."

"Well," he coughed, settling into his tale, in a curious sing-song accent I recognized as hailing from the Antipodes, "life's been good to me of late but it weren't always that way. I've a knack of finding trouble and I reckon I found the worst of it when I met Charlie Higgins. Him and me were inmates on the *Dromedary* – a prison hulk moored off Woolwich. An old fifty-gun, two-decker, made after the Rum Rebellion. Stripped of its masts, rigging, and sails, it was a sorry old beast.

"Now, I ain't a good bloke. I'm a brawler and thief but I believe in paying my dues. That's as much honesty as my old man beat into me. But this place was a floating hell that no human being deserved – and that's the truth of it. Home to six-hundred souls, each with a sleeping space of five-feet-eleven-inches long and eighteen-inches wide – and me six foot tall and a couple more across. In the winter, our blankets froze solid and there were many a mate who ended up just as cold and stiff in the morning. In the summer, we spent our nights choking in the dust and heat below decks, while vermin and disease ate us up. Our days we spent unloading ballast, hefting cables, dredging channels – all the dirty, dangerous work they usually pay the Paddies to do. But we were free labour for the docks. Making rich men richer. And we did it with both ankles chained. Misbehave, and the weight of the leg irons would be increased. It was that what left my mate, Charlie, lame.

"We was in for a year, Charlie and me. Damn near broke us. To this day I have nightmares where I'm wrapped in cold iron, rats eating my face." As he spoke, I saw that big man grow pale, his hands clenching convulsively. He paused, gave a visible judder, and pressed on with his tale.

"At the end of it, no one would look at us or give us honest work. We were sleeping rough, stealing food. Then we fell lucky. I'd been trained as a carpenter and heard Samuel Black was looking for help. So I went along, and he agreed to take me on at half-pay to see how things'd work out. Charlie got some odd jobs for a shop down on Cable Street and it felt like life was on the up.

"Well, Charlie could never keep his eyes off a pretty woman and he gets it into his head that the lady of the house is keen on him. She's laid up in bed awaiting a new baby and, naturally, calling on him to do little errands while her husband's busy. But he sees more to it than that and, once he'd got an idea fixed in his mind, no amount of talking would shake it. Eventually the lady complains to her husband and he's out on his ear. Round the same time, my gaffer found out I'd been in the hulks and that was the end of that.

"Later, I learnt that the sneaky beggar had gone and got himself an apprentice. So he didn't even have to pay half-wages. That got my blood boiling and no mistake. Then Charlie tells me that he never got paid neither, so one thing led to another – us, drinking hard, and the more we talked, and the more we drank, the more it seemed like we were owed. Like I said, I ain't a good bloke and never been averse to a bit of thievery, so it was decided. That night we were going to take what was ours.

"God's honest truth, though, burglary was all I had in mind. I took my maul and chisel thinking we'd maybe need to break open a few strong boxes and the like. But things played out different from how we planned. Very different.

"We arrived at Cable Street gone midnight. A light was still burning in front and I figured, maybe another hour and the whole house would be asleep. But Charlie had his blood up and a sudden mind to have things out with Jameson, so he hammers on the door. The man opened up sharp enough and, after a bit of chat, he let us in.

"At first it was real friendly. He'd just become a father, he said. Let bygones be bygones, he said. Have a drink, he said. Wet the baby's head, he said. But then Charlie starts asking about his misses. Wants to see her, pay his respects. Jameson's edgy, like, and Charlie won't take no for an answer, and pretty soon things start to get heated. He seizes the lantern, pushes his way past the counter and into the back room, heading for the stairs. Jameson follows, grabs him, and the two start to tussle. I get between them, and it's then that things go south.

"There's a boy out back, locking up. He's a thin streak of nothing but he's got gumption. He sees what's going down and makes a grab at Charlie. Takes him by the coat sleeves.

Jameson slips through my outstretched hands and pretty soon, the two of them are hauling Charlie out the back door. All the time, Charlie's yawling like a cat on heat for me to help him.

"By now my blood's pumping, head's spinnin'. I'm panicking about the noise. About the neighbors hearing. Calling the peelers. Putting me back in the hulks. Seems like I can't think straight. All I know is my mate's in trouble and I just do it. I grab the maul that's lying heavy in my jacket and I swing it at the kid. It catches him under the chin and he drops with an 'orrible crunch. Charlie dashes back into the house leavin' just Jameson and me.

"He roars at me and I swing again. And again. And again. It's like I'm watching myself. Like the whole 'orrible nightmare is happening to someone else and I can't stop. Then, suddenly Charlie's back at my my side, pulling me out the door. The maul slips from my hand, slick with brains.

"The rest of the night's a blur. I stumbled out the back door. Fell. Smashed the glass in the little transom window. Sliced my hand right open and didn't even feel it.

"Charlie's pale, gabbling. Says we need a stake. Some money to get away. Start fresh. We haul up, over the back wall, and he leads me through the street. All the time I'm shaking my head like some mad elephant. Trying to clear my thoughts. But all I keep seeing is my maul smashing into the wreckage of that face, over and over.

"We arrive at Black's place. Charlie breaks a window, climbs in, and I follow. The strong box is in Black's room, where him and his wife slept. I lead Charlie up. I figure the apprentice sleeps opposite and I go in to check on him. Make sure he don't raise the alarm. I'd swear on The Bible, that all

I gave was him a little tap. Just enough to put him down but then Charlie reappears and I hear him say 'Saints Alive Davy, you're a murderous beast and no mistake'. And I look down and I see that young boy, lying broken beyond all repair and I knew then that there'd be three ghosts following me to my grave and calling for my damnation.

"So we ran. Ran for hours it seemed. By Sun up, we were on a train bound for Portsmouth. From there we bought passage to Calais. Worked our way as far away as we could from the unholy mess we'd left behind. Ended up in Australia. It was only a few years ago that I learnt what Charlie had done. Those women. That baby. I swear, if I'd known at the time I'd 'ave done fer him myself. But by then he was dead and it was left to me to put things right."

Mathers finally stopped his pacing and looked at Holmes with a sort of hungry desperation.

"And you can do that now, Davy. I have all the proof you need" Holmes whispered as though reluctant to break the spell Mathers' tale had woven. "I have your testimony, confirmation of the all details it has been possible to corroborate, and Abless' thumb imprint to compare with yours. The one taken when we met, and the one on the boy's night-shirt. They match."

Mathers sighed and nodded. "Call the police then. I'll be waiting in my hotel. All I ask is two things. Give Mr. Abless a decent burial. I've money set aside for that that. And you write to my daughter in Adelaide once the courts have done with me. You tell her the truth. The papers are bound to make a sensation of it. Her old dad weren't a good man, but he were a better man for her being in his life and I'd like her to know that."

I sat by the fire long after Mathers had left, deep in thought.

"You believe I should have sent him away? Refused to help?" Holmes eventually asked.

I honestly didn't know. It felt right, that Abless' name would be cleared, that the real murderer would finally face justice, but part of me wondered about Holmes. He had been working for months for a murderer! Invited him into our home, treated him like a guest.

Holmes paused, then nodded thoughtfully.

"To do what I do," he said, "I must separate the crime from the criminal. I can never never let myself be carried away by the heat of the moment. I must be lead by facts. Or I am no better than the magistrate who allowed Able Abless to be hounded to his death."

"But do you not feel …" I began … not all-together sure where my question was heading.

"Yes, Watson, I do feel!" Holmes replied, in a measured tone laced with heat "and I tell you this: Though you may think me an automaton, a calculating-machine, had I a sister, a daughter, or a loved one who had been so cruelly slaughtered I would burn the world to its foundations to uncover the truth. I confess that I might even take the law into my own hands. Yes. I might even do that. Would that, then, be the human, thing to do?

"What of the man who murders the one who kills his wife. He's not an evil man. Not likely to kill ever again. What does the world gain by his death? Should I let him go free?

“What is moral? What is fair? How do I balance justice with vengeance? Is that even my job?

“I have encountered creatures whose very presence fills me with the same creeping sensation as you’d feel watching a python digest a meal. Although I can prove no wrong-doing that any court of law would accept, I know them for the villains they are. But, here, a murder comes to me, confesses his crime, and asks for my help. Do I turn him away in disgust, in horror, or do I seek justice? Not just for his victims, but for the man who has spent forty years in a suicide’s grave for a crime in which he had no part?”

There were no easy answers to Holmes's questions and I confessed as much. But I recalled how Mathers had looked as his left our rooms. A man who, it seemed to me, was curiously light on his feet for someone who was surely walking towards the gallows. And, as I glanced at my friend Sherlock Holmes I knew that, whatever his failings, I could trust him to do what was right.

NOTES

Formed in 1789, the River Police were London’s first police force. Surprisingly, evidence collecting was fairly diligent even in an era of minimal forensics. If not officially, then unofficially, souvenir taking was also common place.

Although Watson has disguised the names of those involved, the brutal Ratcliff Highway murders would have been well known to students of crime. As Holmes relates, the only witness did indeed escape the murderers by climbing from his bedroom window using his bedsheets as a rope. A carpenter’s maul was believed to be one of the murder implements. However, few people genuinely believed that the accused – John Williams – was guilty. Williams was found dead in his cell under suspicious circumstances, and the magistrate in charge had previously been accused of impropriety on an unrelated case. Such was the public outrage at the crimes, Williams' corpse was paraded through the streets before being publicly whipped and interred, at the crossroads, as Holmes describes. Alternative suspects included two men: one lame, the other a seaman called Ablass.

Experiments on pig corpses have shown that quicklime can indeed act as a preservative. Its use in burials is likely to come from the attempts to stop bad smells – the miasmas – which were believed to cause disease.

Dr. Faulds fought long and hard to be recognized for his work on finger-printing. His article in *Nature,* 'On the Skin-Furrows of the Hands', from October 1880, describes the technique used in Watson's account.

The Two Goodly Gentlemen

Truth, they say, is often stranger than fiction – and the events of the evening of March 1st, 1899, were certainly strange. One might even say astonishing.

Holmes was standing before the fire, his face fixed with that singularly introspective air of his. It wasn't unusual for the two of us to sit in companionable silence of an evening, but that night, the heavy air lay around us like a swaddling blanket, and the quiet was broken only by the gentle hiss of gaslight and the crackle of coal in the grate.

We would, perhaps, have spent the next hour or so, warm and content in such fashion, had we not been roused from our reveries by a hammering on the street door, followed in quick succession by eager voices, a heavy tread on the stairs, and a knock on our door.

The man who entered was round shouldered and pale – his silhouette made heavier by the addition of a Newmarket waterproof, with its collar pulled up to keep out the damp. He paused on the threshold. Then, taking off his bowler, stepped into the room.

Neither the gloom nor our visitor's precautions against the weather prevented Holmes from recognizing our unexpected guest.

"Why, Hopkins!" Holmes said, sounding genuinely delighted. "Whatever brings you to Baker Street on such a filthy night?"

Inspector Stanley Hopkins was an eminently practical detective who Holmes had taken quite the shine to. Hopkins, in turn, clearly admired Holmes, and had invited him to consult on some of our most interesting cases.

Hopkins paused long enough before replying to pique my companion's curiosity and, in those seconds, Holmes switched seamlessly from a state of dreamy languor into one of nervous alacrity.

"Please, Inspector," he said, "help yourself to a little warmer from the spirit cabinet and tell us what events have left one of Scotland Yard's most-seasoned bulldogs so shaken."

"I'll take that drink with thanks, Mr. Holmes. As you know, I'm not a man in whom emotions run high, but what I've seen tonight has left me fair sick to the stomach – and that's the truth. But as to the *what's* and the *wherefore's*, I fear I haven't the words. You'd best come see for yourself."

We chose to walk rather than wait on a cab, the brisk pace providing welcome warmth against the evening chill.

Our jaunt took us winding through the backstreets to a dainty row of houses just off the Edgware Road. Once known as Wattling Street, this road had carried both Boudicca's warriors and Caesar's centurions through the capital and was now a bustling and thoroughly metropolitan thoroughfare.

The buildings here were mainly five-story brick affairs, with small shops and eateries at street level, large apartments above, and smaller attic rooms perched in neat Dutch gables.

It wasn't long before we spotted the uniformed officers – so distinctive in their custodian helmets – and, huddled in doorways along the streets, small crowds of the curious and the concerned.

The largest of these groups was a collection of young girls who stood shivering under thin shawls, their faces pinched with worry. It was quickly ascertained that the girls belonged to a building whose frontage was lined with tiny cracked windows, giving the impression of a mouth grimacing through splintered teeth.

On closer inspection, this proved to be a workshop of sorts, and the young girls to be seamstresses. It was they who had first noticed it – a slick oily substance, running down the windows of the shop, leaving sickly yellow stains behind, like the trail of some grotesque slug.

The stench here was incredible, as though someone had lit a bucketful of the foulest tallow candles and poured the residue over the whole pavement. It was slick with it.

By the guttering gaslight, it was possible to see that the curious substance emanated not from the storerooms directly above the factory, but from the uppermost level of the inn next door. The liquid had simply found the path of least resistance, from the gable-end window, through cracked bricks and worn mortar, to the street below.

The young ladies were keen to tell us all they knew and Holmes, seeming to them to represent a higher authority than the constables, was quickly inundated with information.

That evening, they said, they had been gathered around the windows, trying to spare the gas. Suddenly there came a series of loud thumps, which quite set them on edge. This was followed by a sudden downpour of terrible fluid, and a stench so suffocating and unnatural-seeming that they quite lost their nerve.

Luckily, the lamplighter was prompt about his business. Sunset was at twenty-to-six that evening, and it was as the light from the street lamp flooded the workroom that they saw that what they had took for rain was in fact a strange oily substance trickling down the window. It was as they were wondering what could be the cause of such an odd occurrence that they heard the landlord of The Sapper's Friend, next door, calling for assistance. The first constables had arrived within minutes.

"And now it looks like we will be cooling our heels here all bloomin' night" one girl complained, peering from under her bonnet at Holmes. "If we don't finish this order, no telling what will happen."

Holmes was ever the gentleman where the fairer sex was concerned. "Can we not let these poor ladies back to their work?" he asked, looking to Hopkins.

"We thought it best to clear the inn and all adjoining properties until we had a better idea of what we were dealing with," the Inspector explained. "There's lots of small businesses hereabouts. Printers, chemists, ladies cosmetics, and the like, all dealing in toxic or combustible materials. I left the constables checking the properties when I came to Baker Street. If they've found nothing untoward, then certainly. Unless, that is . . . ."

Holmes, who had been scanning the rooftops as Hopkins spoke and shook his head distractedly. "No, no. Clearly the inn holds something rather more startling than rain and bumps in the night! Shall we, Inspector?"

The Sapper's Friend bore the image of a flaming grenade above its door, its polished brass and stained glass a literal shining testament to the owner's pride in his establishment.

The landlord, staff, and his patrons were huddled outside where they'd been corralled by a trio of uniformed officers. Hopkins ushered them inside, and gave one of the constables orders not to let anyone leave.

Thanks to numerous pastille burners smoldering gently on the window frames, the smell was, thankfully, considerably sweeter inside than it was outside.

As we climbed the increasingly narrow stairway towards the top floor, however, the smell that had so offended us in the street returned with a vengeance, and Holmes and I were forced to use handkerchiefs to avoid choking on the stench.

We finally reached the top floor, where Hopkins opened the door. There, inside, we could see that a table had been set for two. Earlier in the day, it must have looked a charming room. It was small, warm, and brightly lit, with mirrors on the walls to reflect the candle light.

According to Hopkins, the landlord had provided his patrons with a pot of coffee and a cold collation at three-thirty. The door had been locked to assure the guests of the absolute privacy they'd requested, and remained so until the landlord arrived with brandy and fresh coffee at five-thirty precisely.

Holmes's bright eyes took in the room and its hideous contents. He looked calm enough, but the hand he had placed on my shoulder gripped me like a vice.

“Before we go any further – Watson, Hopkins, tell me, quickly: What do you smell? Don’t think about it. Close your eyes and tell me the first words that come to mind.”

“Liver and onions” I said.

“Bacon and cabbage” Hopkins added.

“Interesting. Thank you. Please, proceed.”

We entered the room, where a curious plume of carbon hung in the air over the table where the patrons still sat. Or rather, I should say, what remained of them. For there, on the elegantly carved chairs, were the empty clothes of two men. Their feet were still in their boots, but of the rest of their bodies, there was no sign. It was as if they had been consumed by some miraculous conflagration which had left clothes, chairs, and surrounding fabrics unburnt, while reducing their mortal remains to soot.

“But where’s the rest of them, Mr. Holmes?” Hopkins asked in a tone of quiet awe. “That’s what I want to know. Where’s the rest of them?”

There could be no doubt. Holmes voiced it before I could, but I could tell that we had reached the same frightful conclusion at the same time. “Imagine these gentlemen as human candles, and what you have here,” he gestured towards the floor with a grimace, “is the residue. Water – we are mostly water, after all – and human fat, rendered into oil by the application of great heat. You’re standing in them, Inspector. We all are.”

Holmes, Hopkins, and I were no strangers to death in all its curious forms, but it’s fair to say that none of us wanted to remain a second longer than necessary in that charnel house.

Despite that, my companion insisted on a thorough examination of the scene.

"So at five-thirty," Holmes said, voicing his thoughts, "the landlord unlocked the door. The horror he felt can be no less than our own, for the tray – loaded with a brandy decanter and glasses – was dropped by the open door. Despite that initial shock, he clearly attempted to open the windows. You can see his footprints in the greasy slick, and on the table cloth where he wiped his hands of the oil that covers the window frame, in order to get better purchase. We can assume he gave up because the casement is still secure. He then opened the closure plate on the fire – again, his greasy finger marks are quite clear. No need to wonder why, given the stench. On his way out, he appears to have cleared the dropped tray and removed the lunch leftovers from the sideboard. The serving dishes are gone."

"Lord!" I said. "He must have quite a strong stomach, our landlord, to stop to tidy up!"

Holmes said nothing, but began sniffing at the charcoaled remains with huge exaggerated inhales. He started at those horrible booted feet and worked his way up like a blood-hound taken human form.

"And it would seem that the landlord isn't the only one with a strong stomach," I said, aghast. "What on earth are you doing?"

"Come here, Watson, and tell me what you can smell?"

"Again? Must I?"

I leaned over the charred offerings, thankful that I hadn't yet had supper, and did as Holmes had done – and took a deep breath.

"Rust."

Holmes gave just the whisper of a smile. "Very pungent, isn't it?"

"That isn't unusual, given the amount of blood in a human body."

"Mmm. But smell the rest of the seat."

I did so and was surprised at the result. "Nothing." I said.

"How likely would it be for the blood in a burning body to pool in just one spot like this?" Holmes said, a tense whisper.

"Ordinarily, pooling is rare without some underlying vascular issue. If a person was lying unconscious for a long period of time – as happens with comatose patients – then blood would pool in those areas in direct contact with the bed or say, in this case, the chair. But then the whole seat would be infused with blood. Not just one spot."

"Thank you. Just as I thought."

Holmes prowled the room, occasionally stopping to hum or scratch his chin in some perplexity. Eventually he headed to the window, which yielded to the application of force, allowing gusts of blissfully fresh night air to clear the ghastly odor.

For a while my companion remained hanging out of the window, and my imagination – inflamed by the macabre surroundings – led to the horrible fancy that his torso was entirely headless.

He was eventually called back in by Hopkins, who had been examining two large trunks in the corner of the private dining room. "Odd," he said, motioning Holmes and me to come closer. "See how the bails of cloth at the top of the trunks have been unrolled and left higgedly-piggedly? Yet below are single pieces of cloth, all still neatly folded. And look how they have been crushed down, as though a great weight has been placed on top. The same is true for both trunks."

"Something has been removed?" I asked. "And the bails unrolled to hide their loss?"

"Certainly," Holmes said with the look of a delinquent schoolboy harboring a secret he could barely contain. It was a look I knew of old. By Jove! He was on to something!

"Should we assume that the murders were committed to hide a theft?" Hopkins asked. "Or was the murderer an opportunist?"

"What makes you think it's murder?" Holmes said.

"Well, if it's an accident, I've never seen the like," the inspector replied, sounding a little queasy as contemplated the evening's events. "A fire in a shuttered room that burnt two bodies, and nothing more! Why didn't the men call for help as soon as the fire caught? And why didn't the whole blessed room go up?"

"Excellent questions, Inspector!" Holmes said, in the sort of excited tones that only he would ever use for such a gruesome topic. "When you set a body alight, it first pyrolyzes into carbon. Some subcutaneous fats will begin to melt at one-hundred degrees. Fires that start this way tend to burn slowly, and straight up, scorching the ceiling, but leaving the surroundings intact. The question is: How does one generate the temperatures involved in rendering bone to dust outside of a regenerative furnace?"

"A what?" Hopkins asked.

"A crematorium."

"Unless . . ." Holmes trailed off.

"Unless?" I prompted.

". . . Unless you believe in spontaneous human combustion."

His response was so surprising that I couldn't help but laugh. "And do you?" I asked.

"Well, the wick effect, where the human body becomes its own source of fuel – burning to great temperatures – has been widely observed."

"But that's incredible!" I protested.

"Incredible, yes. Improbable, yes. But impossible? Let us say, not yet proven. But come – this is too foul a place for clear thinking. Let us see what our remarkably strong-stomached landlord has to say for himself."

It's long been my whimsy that British army sergeants are chosen purely because they're the biggest, toughest, most bull-headed men in the regiment. Sergeant Knowles, therefore, proved to be quite the surprise. He was a man in his late forties, small and wiry, with unmanageable pepper-grey curls, and keen eyes that regarded us – and me especially, it seemed – with interest.

He ushered us behind the bar to a back room that served as both office and lounge. A small cylinder desk and high stool occupied one corner, with bookshelves floor to ceiling, and a cozy-looking armchair beside the fire.

Holmes stood back and let Hopkins lead the examination, which he began by asking about the gentlemen who had hired the dining room. Knowles proved to be a willing, if laconic, witness.

"The room was reserved for Saville Gittins," he said. "His business associate was George Mannings. The room was booked and paid for in advance. The gents arrived in good order and headed straight for the apartment. My girl, Sally, had already laid out cold meats, bread, and cheese, along with a spirit burner filled with coffee, as I'd received orders that, once the door was locked, they were not to be disturbed.

"Did you know them?"

"They were regulars. Like a lot of the patrons here, ex-military. You know how it is: There's a bond between men who've served. They were fine men, I'd say."

"Was it their habit to reserve a room for business?"

"No. First time."

"And what was that business?"

"Military surplus. They bought up old uniforms, blankets, and the like and refashioned them into cheap clothing. The factory next door was theirs."

"Address?"

"They live above the factory, I believe."

"Family?"

"Mannings' elderly parents were recently carried off by the influenza. There was no one else I knew of."

Hopkins licked his pencil thoughtfully, scribbling Knowles' comments into his notebook before waving him to continue.

"I locked the door myself and knew no more about it until that terrible hour. I had loaded a tray and was at the door as the hour hit its halfway mark. But I could smell it almost as soon as I began to climb the stairs. I've been in battle,

Inspector. I know the stench of cooked flesh when I encounter it, so I opened up in quick time."

"Describe it, please, Mr. Knowles," interrupted Holmes. "The smell."

"Well, it's nothing like pork. That's what you'll read. There's an element of that, no doubt. What I got first off – were the high notes, so to speak."

"The blood?" Holmes said.

"Just so. See, humans aren't pigs. At least they're not pork, which comes prepared, and dressed, and ready for eating. Human bodies still have blood inside them. And brains. And all their organs. Burn them, and what you get is a hot metal smell. That's the blood. Then a musky, sweet perfume. That's the brains. Then burnt liver. That's the organs. The flesh. That's the sickly smell that lingers."

As Knowles spoke, Hopkins visibly paled, but Holmes was in his element.

"Outstanding, Mr. Knowles. Outstanding! So you opened the door, and got quite the shock, I imagine?"

"I should say so! Took me right back to Kandahar. Smoke and death. Thought I was done with all that."

My ears pricked up at learning that Knowles, like myself, was another remnant of the Afghan War. Still, regardless of that avowed "bond between men who've served", I couldn't help but feel something was 'off' with the sergeant's account of events.

"Forgive me," I asked. "Which regiment were you with?"

"Royal Engineers."

"Ah, I see!" I exclaimed. "The Sapper's Friend!"

"That's right. Did my time. Then did a spell at the Royal Arsenal. Good pay and interesting work, but there comes a point in his life when a man yearns to be his own boss – and my brother-in-law's in the pub trade. Seemed like an honest way to earn a living. Been at it just over a year now."

As Holmes listened to our exchange, it was as though I could actually see the connections being made in his brain. Something Knowles had said had caught his attention.

"Continue, please" he said.

"Well, I saw the carbon in the air and feared the whole establishment was about to go up, so I dropped everything, extinguished all the flames – the pastille burners and the spirit burner – and then ran to the fireplace to open it up and get some air in."

"You opened the window?"

"I tried to," the landlord said, all the time seeming to hold myself as his fixed point of attention. "Couldn't budge it."

I could see Holmes examining Knowles for those tell-tale signs that even the most habitual liars exhibit. Several times during Knowles' statement, I saw him give a flicker of a smile. Only those who know Holmes intimately would have spotted it, but I fancied that he had caught the landlord in some untruth. "Why did you remove the food?" he asked.

Knowles shrugged. "Can't abide mess."

Hopkins chipped in. "You prepare all the food here?"

"We do."

"We'll need to take what's left of the lunch away for analysis." Hopkins told him.

"Good luck with that," the landlord answered in those terse military tones of his. "I fed it to the dogs. Seemed a shame to let good food go to waste." Then he added, almost as an afterthought, "Look, now, it seems to me that there's a question you're not asking. Let's have it, then."

"It's this, Mr. Knowles," the inspector said. "Someone burnt two men to death in a room to which only you had the key. Let us say they were drugged and set alight. Let us say that those drugs were in the food. Or maybe there was some soporific in the spirit burner. You see how it looks?"

"I do," Knowles replied looking remarkably self-contained, "but what would I have to gain from such an act?"

"Well," the inspector replied, "that's the question, isn't it? Tell me about the trunks. Did you take them up to the room?"

"I did."

"No other staff helped?"

"No."

"Do you know what was in the trunks?"

"Samples, I'd been told."

"Did you open them?"

"No."

"Were they open when you entered the room?"

"Can't say."

Hopkins sighed, frustrated by Knowles' increasingly terse replies. "All right, Mr. Knowles. We'll need to speak to your staff and patrons. Tell the officer in the saloon to give me ten minutes then start sending them through."

Knowles headed off to do as he'd been asked, allowing Hopkins to express his annoyance with the lack of information being volunteered. "I'm half-inclined to take Knowles down to the station, if only for his alarming knowledge of how human bodies burn. What would you say to that, Mr. Holmes?"

"I'd say," Holmes replied, "that Mr. Knowles is unlikely to volunteer anything that he doesn't want us to know. I assume the constables are already taking statements from the neighbors?"

Hopkins nodded.

"Good. You stay here and speak to the staff and customers. Watson and I will try our luck next door and see if I can't track down that lamplighter."

"And what about you, Doctor?" Hopkins asked. "Any thoughts?"

"Only that our landlord reads far too many lurid novels."

"Oh?" Hopkins and Holmes said in unison.

"Precisely" I said, pointing to the bookshelf. "He has quite the collection."

"Yellow jackets?" Holmes smiled. "Hardly on your level, Watson!"

I confess I flushed up with pleasure at his words. "To my mind," I said, "Knowles may have been in the military long-enough to have acquired a certain level-headed veneer, but his bookshelf tells quite a different tale. He has quite the fanciful taste in literature. Here we have *Frankenstein.* Here *Udolpho*." I noted that, in a row dedicated to detective fiction, there were even some of my own reminiscences, which perhaps explained his interest in my person. "There's something else too: *Bleak House*."

Again: "Oh?"

I shouldn't have been surprised that neither Holmes nor Hopkins were not completely familiar with the works of one of Britain's most celebrated novelists. "Charles Dickens. It contains quite a famous scene. A character called Krook dies – by bursting into flames!"

Hopkins looked likely to have a paroxysm. "Lord, not that again! And here I was thinking this whole thing was strange enough as a simple robbery and murder, without throwing magic into the mix!"

Holmes merely smiled that small, knowing smile. "We'll reconvene at Baker Street," he said. "Please be so kind as to bring Knowles along. Two hours should be sufficient to clear this case up. Oh, and Hopkins – if you could send a telegram to the local constabularies along the Kings Cross-to-Wales line, that would be most helpful."

"You think the perpetrator is on the run then?"

"I do."

"And do you have a description of the man in question?" Hopkins asked, sounding skeptical.

"No," my companion replied, "but I'm sure the customers will be able to supply you with descriptions of both Mannings and Gittins." With that, he turned on his heels and headed into the night.

I often think that if Holmes hadn't turned that remarkable mind of his to the science of detection, he would have made a fine actor. He had the thespian's love of the dramatic, and was never happier than when he was holding stage, revealing those truths which seemed so clear to him, but so obscure to us lesser mortals.

Hopkins arrived exactly two hours after we had left him at The Sapper's Friend, with Knowles in custody, if not actually in handcuffs.

"Ah, Inspector. Mr. Knowles," Holmes said, sounding as though he was greeting a much-loved maiden aunt. "Please be seated. Now, Inspector, what did you discover from the staff and patrons?"

Hopkins gave a little cough to acknowledge the courtesy. "Neither staff nor guests could add much to the account of the evening's events," he said. "But according to the barmaid, Sally, Knowles, Mannings, and Gittins were more than casual acquaintances. "Firm friends" is how she described them. Mannings had held the wake for his parents at the pub, with Knowles footing the bill. She said it was an act of kindness because "everyone knew the factory was in trouble" and they were "goodly gentlemen". A few days after the wake, she'd seen both Mannings and Gittins in the main bar with another gent. Gossip was that they were about to sell up, but guessing the direction you were going in, Mr. Holmes, I got the gentleman's name from one of the regulars. It's a local's local – everyone knows everyone – so it didn't take much digging. I've sent a constable to find him and send him our way. But come, Mr. Holmes, I know that this is just the side-dish to the meat of the thing. Your fine mind has uncovered much more than my plodding ever could. So if you would oblige me, I'm eager to hear what it is that I've missed."

Holmes waved away the compliment, unfolded himself from his chair and, warming his spare frame in front of the fire, began.

"It was well done, Mr. Knowles. Very well done. Where you went wrong was in being a little too theatrical. I suspect we have Mr. Dickens to blame for that."

"I don't know what you think you know," Knowles said confidently, "but I can tell you, I've committed no crime."

"We shall see, Mr. Knowles. Much depends on what our new visitor has to say."

I hadn't heard any footsteps on the stair, but a knock, followed by the entrance of a short, pock-faced man, confirmed Holmes's statement.

The man looked a little alarmed at finding himself in a room full of people whose attentions were now directed entirely at himself. "I was instructed to present myself to Inspector Hopkins," the man said in reedy voice, made the more timorous by the strangeness of the situation.

"Come in, come in. We won't keep you but a few moments, Mr. – ?"

"Timson," the timorous man said, "of Timson and Sons, Insurance Brokers."

"Mr. Timson, no need for alarm. Inspector Hopkins of Scotland Yard is investigating the deaths of two men – a Mr. Mannings and Mr. Gittins. We just have a few questions about a policy they took with you. Just a formality, you understand, and then you're free to leave. I'm sure that you have better places to be."

The insurance broker gave a series of nervous little nods. "They were good men," he intoned. "Very good men. And I was honored to cover them for five-thousand apiece."

"Good men, indeed. So we have been told. And who were the beneficiaries?"

"Once all debts had been paid, the seamstresses." Timson said.

"Ha!" Holmes cried, looking both surprised and delighted. "Please note that Inspector. Mr. Timson, you've been of great help!" He steered the baffled man towards the door with a mite more force than necessary before adding, rather apologetically, "Please don't let us detain you!"

Holmes waited for the sound of the street door being closed before he continued.

"Now, as to the events in question," Holmes, said, clearly enjoying his moment in the spotlight, "I'll confess that, the more I was told about how goodly Messers Mannings and Gittins were, the more I was inclined to think that they were the most abject villains. I suspected all sorts of nefarious motives, but it appears, Mr. Knowles, that I owe you an apology. Whatever your involvement, I am sure now that everything was done with the best intentions.

"The seamstresses confirmed that the business had been struggling for some time. As Timson said, these were good men. Good soldiers, too, by all accounts. Sadly, however, not good business men. But they'd taken on debt rather than lay off staff, because they knew that many of the young girls they employed provided the only incomes for their families. In turn, the ladies were attempting to make their own cost-savings, bless them, by limiting gas usage and working extra hours, unpaid, to finish orders ahead of time.

"I believe that the death of Mannings' parents was the spark for a scheme which likely came from the over-active imagination of Mr. Knowles here.

“My first clue was the smell. When Knowles rather ghoulishly described the effects of fire on a human body, he forgot one thing: Burning bodies do indeed smell of iron, but embalmed bodies are first drained of blood. Hence the fact that the only metallic scent in the room was to be found on the seat of each chair. That, and the faint whiff of formaldehyde on the feet, told me all I needed to know.

“I cannot imagine how difficult it must have been to carry out the grim task of squeezing the embalmed bodies of Mannings’ parents into the trunks before dressing them and setting them on fire. The seamstresses heard Mannings and Gittins make their escape across the roof into their own rooms, above the factory. You see, Knowles didn’t try to open the window. He *closed* it. The lamplighter confirmed that. I suspected that he would have line-of-sight from the top of his ladder – and he did. He saw the window lying open as he lit the lamp on Homer Street. That also allowed the rather unpleasant remains of Mr. and Mrs. Mannings to dissipate into the street. The food, of course, had to be removed because it hadn’t been eaten.”

“But this is all too incredible!” I cried. “And what of the fire? How was it done?”

“I knew almost immediately that some incendiary device had been used,” my friend said, “but what? Knowles had been a sapper, and worked munitions at Arsenal. If anyone would know of a way to burn bodies without burning the surrounding environment, I was sure he would. The evidence suggested something containing iron oxide, which had left such a strong scent on the chairs. Then I remembered the Goldschmidt process, which gives off an enormous amount of heat as a result of the chemical combination of aluminum with iron oxides. Yes, thermite paste would easily supply the energy needed, with no perceptible residue other than a smell of rust where the devices were placed."

If Knowles betrayed himself with some twitch or flicker of the eye, I didn't observe it. Indeed, throughout Holmes's exposition, he maintained the appearance of a man of clear conscience.

"Why, thank you, Mr. Holmes!" Hopkins said. "I did at least notice the luggage labels on the trunks, indicating regular trips to the Principality. And Gittins is a Welsh name. Still, we've heard nothing back from our colleagues across the border."

Holmes looked from Hopkins to Knowles and then across the room to where I sat, by the table, with notebook in hand. "You're a fine detective, Hopkins, and I don't doubt that should you decide to pursue this case to the full extent of your powers, you would soon track down the errant men. You may even be able to build a case against Knowles here, although proving he did anything beyond reading lurid literature may be difficult. For what do we really have? No murder. No theft. And arson would imply that Knowles had something to gain, which he didn't. There is no crime in stealing dead bodies, only their personal effects, which would also be nearly impossible to prove . . . ."

"Insurance fraud is a serious crime," Hopkins said.

"I will not say otherwise," Holmes answered, "but I cannot help but think that should Mr. Gittins and Mr. Mannings stay dead, what is the worse that could happen? Their debtors would be happy. Their employees would be happy. The customers of Timson and Timson may see their premiums increase by, what? A penny or a ha'penny. This is entirely your case, Inspector, but a ha'penny seems a small cost for such happiness, don't you think?"

Hopkins picked up his bowler and, regarding the rim, thoughtfully began to wipe it free from imaginary dust. Then, he popped it on his head and made for the door. "I'll keep you abreast of any developments," he said.

We watched Hopkins leave, and then sat warming ourselves for a while as Holmes poured drinks.

"What now?" Knowles eventually asked.

"Oh, Hopkins is also a good man," Holmes said. "I suspect this little adventure is unlikely to find its way into the good Doctor's annals."

I thought that maybe Knowles looked a little sorry at that, but he still managed to raise a glass and a smile all the same.

NOTES

Termite was patented in 1895. The process would eventually be used on the railways to weld railway tracks together. Its inventor, Hans Goldschmidt, published several extensive papers on the process during 1898, including an article in *The Journal of the Society of Chemical Industry* which both Holmes and Knowles, with their professional interest in such things, may have been familiar with. However, various high-temperature welding processes were also known from the 1880s, and may equally have provided the heat needed to to burn the bodies so throughly.

Spontaneous human combustion was topic of fascination to both writers and scientists during the Victorian era. Melville (1849) and Dickens (1853) both used it, somewhat sensationally, as a literary device. Scientific studies were unable to prove that such fires started 'spontaneously' but even the *British Medical Journal* (1888, "Case of So-Called 'Spontaneous Combustion'"by J. Mackenzie Booth) discussed the possible conditions which might make such combustion possible. It was, however, acknowledged that bodies could burn in such a startling fashion given the right source of ignition.

Pigs bodies, set alight, tend to create fires that burn straight up, singing the ceiling, while leaving the most of the surroundings intact. These fires burn slowly, leaving a greasy residue of liquefied fat behind. In humans, it's likely that the hands and feet are left behind, as they are relatively fat-free.

The Backwater Affair

Glancing over my records of all the cases in which I have assisted my great friend, Sherlock Holmes, I am struck by the number of times that we have been faced with events which, at first, seem to have no natural explanation. I have said before that Holmes worked not for wealth or prestige, but for the sheer thrill of exercising that singular mind of his. Perhaps this is why he especially sought out the bizarre and the fantastical. Or perhaps it was Holmes himself who acted as a magnet for such things? My friend would, of course, dismiss such a concept, but when I look back at my notes from October 1885, the oddness of the events which were to unfold still strikes me.

Winter already had its grip on our little corner of Baker Street. Snow had fallen overnight – a rare sight in London – and a genuine curiosity so early in the year. I awoke to find ice clinging to the inside of the sash windows and the smell of mildew hanging in the air.

I had only just lit the fire when the door to Holmes's bedroom opened. My surprise at seeing my friend awake so early was doubled at the sight of him already dressed.

"Ah, Watson! As reliable as a metronome," he intoned, clearly in good humor. "I hope you will not object to making a speedy toilet this morning. It seems we are to expect visitors." He pulled a crumpled telegram from his jacket pocket and held it out for me to peruse. "It arrived some hours ago. I should warn you that Mrs. Hudson was not best pleased to be awakened before dawn. I wouldn't wait on breakfast."

The telegram gave no me clues as to what – or who – I should expect. "No name? No hints as to who sent it, then?" I asked.

"Government, naturally" Holmes answered with a familiar smile. "Notice how the message is exactly nine words long – penny-pinching officialdom if ever I saw it. Sent from Whitehall, which tells us nothing in itself, but given that only the military mind would willingly rouse itself at such an ungodly hour, and the fact that the Navy Office is situated on The Mall, I'd say we are to expect a visit from The Right Honorable the Lord Backwater, First Lord of the Admiralty."

"Know the man?" I asked.

"I've heard of him. In the best traditions of British bureaucracy, he has never set foot on a ship, boat, or punt. Highly strung. Considered to be the type to 'get things done' – which, between the two of us, is likely Admiralty code for someone who makes a lot of unnecessary work for others!"

Holmes was proved entirely correct. At exactly seven a.m., the spare and skittish figure of Phillip George Lorling, 1st Earl of Backwater, Liberal statesman and head of Her Majesty's Navy, entered our sitting room and was ushered towards the battered sofa upon which Holmes habitually lay when in the grip of a particularly knotty problem.

From his wild, untamed hair to his cross-buttoned overcoat, Backwater seemed like a man in a hurry. It was only when I had drawn shut the curtains on the windows and checked that the door to the apartment was securely locked that he could be compelled to sit down at all. "Security," he said in a high, timorous whine. "One can never be too careful."

As I lit the lamp, Holmes made himself comfortable in his easy chair and said, in the soothing tones that he employed so well, "Please start at the beginning. And leave out no detail, no matter how strange it should appear."

At this, our visitor visibly started and looked at Holmes inquiringly.

"No magic I assure you. It's rare for people to consult with me on mundane matters. In fact, Watson believes that I have a knack for attracting the uncanny . . . ." He let his sentence trail off and, with a wave of his hand, motioned our visitor to begin.

Backwater spoke quickly with a tense edge to his voice which was reflected in his body language.

"You will know that I am but newly appointed to the Admiralty. I'm a modern man, Mr. Holmes, and am determined to bring much needed order to the department. Paper – or rather velum I should say – lines the very corridors, and much of my time, thus far, has been spent following paper trails. It was one such trail that led me to a discovery that I believe may imperil the Empire herself."

He paused to glance around the room, then continued in the same oddly strained tone. "In 1850, a private gentlemen – his name is not recorded – saw a paragraph in a newspaper which, although couched in a very guarded manner, attracted his observation. After making enquiries at the newspaper office, he was introduced to someone who called himself 'Captain Werner'. Of particular note was that, during the last war, he had been in the employ of the Government. He is said to have used a small submersible to destroy a French gunship. As an aside here, Mr. Holmes, a gunship was destroyed under

– shall we say – strange circumstances during this time, but we have no records of any Captain Werner on our pay books.

"This same gentleman now asserted to have invented a device which was capable of destroying any ship, from a distance, on command. Well, Mr. Holmes, it seems that Werner had friends in Parliament, and they raised a request with the House to fund a trial of this remarkable invention."

"Did such a trial take place?" Holmes asked.

"It seems so. At least there are records of a hulk, called the *John O' Gaunt*, moored in deep waters off Gladwyn Sands, which was destroyed by means unknown. After the demonstration, Werner apparently demanded £200,000 for the secret."

"An incredible sum!" I interjected, unable to stifle my surprise.

"His supporters felt it wasn't unreasonable, given that anyone owning such a device could potentially destroy any ship, any harbor, anywhere."

"Was he paid?" Holmes asked quietly.

"I believe so – "

"Believe?" Holmes barked. "That's quite a sum for the Admiralty to lose!"

"Yes," Lord Backwater answered brittlely. "Yes. He was paid the amount requested. You must understand," he added, as though he felt the need to personally justify such a fabulous expense, "that great ideas have always incurred ridicule. After all, the man who introduced gas, from which we all derive so much benefit, died in a debtor's prison."

"Just so," said Holmes, holding up a placating hand. "Pray continue."

"I have ascertained from reading the Parliamentary records in Hansard that negotiations rumbled on. When it became clear that Werner intended to offer his device to the Portuguese, the issue was referred to the Duke – Wellington you understand – who personally appointed two officers to make a detailed report. Their findings were strongly in favor of securing the device for the country."

"Did it not occur to anyone," Holmes hazarded, "that the British Government was being hoodwinked, possibly with the aid of these officers?"

Lord Backwater scowled. "Reports were made in writing, supported by numerous witnesses to both Werner's character and the efficiency of the device. There was seemingly abundant evidence to support their decision. That, and a year's constant intercourse between the Duke and Captain Werner, was considered sufficient proof of his good intentions."

"Well, one can have friends in high places and still be a scoundrel. So a king's ransom was paid for the plans to this miraculous device. Did it live up to expectations?"

"In all honesty, Mr. Holmes, I can find no one who has any knowledge of the thing. Captain Werner died after delivering the plans. The officers who made the original report were posted overseas and are now long dead, as is the Duke. The plans themselves simply vanished."

The room fell silent. Holmes regarded Backwater thoughtfully then leaned forward. "It is hard to imagine that the Government, having spent such a vast sum, simply dropped the matter. Were no investigations made at the time?"

"Naturally. Clerks were set to scour the archives in case the plans had been misfiled. Mrs. Hannah Chesters – a lady of independent means whose husband financed some of Werner's work – was interviewed. But she claimed that Werner alone held the secret. The matter was raised again in the Lords, then abandoned."

"How very curious." Holmes eventually said, peering at Backwater with those steady grey eyes of his.

"Mr. Holmes," Lord Backwater answered with a wan smile, "I don't believe that this is a case of fraud, if that's what you're implying. But officials have a long and noble history of burying embarrassing mistakes. Payment was made. A document was logged, archived, then 'lost'. An empty file is all that is left to show for two-hundred-thousand of public money."

"So you wish me to recover the plans for device?"

Backwater didn't answer immediately, and when he did it was in a curiously thoughtful tone. "While, of course, the recovery of these plans would be of immense value to the Empire – and a feather in my cap – it is another question that I find vexes and unnerves me.

"I cannot abide mysteries, Mr. Holmes. I must have things ordered and quantified. It is the only way for a modern man to live, don't you agree?"

I could see Holmes, who was by no means an ordered man himself, appraising Backwater with just the hint of a smile, but he said nothing.

"Things that defy reason cause me sleepless nights," the First Lord continued. "Assuming the device is genuine – and I have read enough to convince me that it is – and assuming it was stolen, why have we not seen it used by our enemies? If someone is holding the plans for their own purposes, surely thirty-five years is time enough? And exactly how was it taken? How was someone able to walk into a locked safe, in the basement of Whitehall's most secure and heavily-guarded rooms? What have I missed, Mr. Holmes? That is the real mystery that I wish you to solve for me. Come by tomorrow – you'll doubtless want to see the strong room for yourself – and I will ensure what records we have are put at your disposal."

The street door had barely closed before Holmes was bounding across the room pulling out files and newspaper clippings, and spreading them across the woefully empty breakfast table.

"Come, Watson, don't look so downcast!" he said. "If I'm not mistaken, that's Mrs. Hudson's queenly tread I hear on the stairs. And if can't smell fresh rashers and hot coffee, then you have my permission to call me a humbug if I ever boast of my olfactory prowess again!"

Sure enough, the door opened and in came our redoubtable landlady with not just bacon and coffee, but eggs and toast. "Given the early start," she said, with just the hint of reproach, "I assumed you would be in need of a good breakfast before you head out to Heaven knows where."

I loaded an appreciatively large plate and sat down to eat while Holmes scattered papers over table and floor, in a vigorous imitation of the snowfall outside. Finally, he held up a small manila folder with a triumphant flourish.

"Ah, here we are," he began. "An obituary from 1880 for Hannah Chesters – the woman mentioned by Backwater. She was single at the time of her death, residing at number 10 Wilton Crescent, Belgrave Square. Former housekeeper to John

Chesters, with whom she had three children. She had taken Chesters' last name, and upon his death, Hannah – housekeeper and mistress – inherited the bulk of his vast fortune. The inheritance was hotly contested by Chesters' actual wife, who claimed that her husband wasn't of sound mind when he re-wrote his will in favor of Hannah, the mistress. Apparently it was a *cause célèbre* at the time. The judge decided in the mistress' favor, but the lady opted to share the bequest with the wife, on the condition that her own young daughters were well provided for."

"Sounds like an interesting lady," I said between mouthfuls of hot, buttered toast.

"Interesting couple. According to this clipping, Hannah and John were buried in a rather striking pyramid-shaped mausoleum in Brompton. Apparently Mr. Chesters had a passion for Egyptology."

"Academic or amateur?"

"Unknown. In fact, no one seems to know exactly how he made his fortune."

"Chesters' real wife?"

"Dead for some time."

"Any mention of Werner?"

"None."

Holmes handed me the clipping. Alongside a portrait of the late Hannah Chesters was an illustration of the door of an imposing mausoleum, its surround decorated with *ankh*-shapes and hieroglyphics.

"Interesting, but it's a bit thin" I said, loathe to dampen Holmes's enthusiasm.

"It is" he replied, with a look of impish pleasure settling onto his features. The game – as he so often said –was afoot.

We arrived at that monument to officialdom and paper-shuffling – the Admiralty – the next morning, just as Big Ben's distinctive quarter-bells sounded the first division of the hour. The building lacks its own entrance on The Mall, meaning that visitors must cross Horse Guard's Parade where, as the name suggests, the Queen's official bodyguards are put through their daily maneuvers.

The First Lord has rooms on the upper floor, but instead of being escorted to his apartments as expected, Holmes and I found ourselves whisked down several flights of worn steps into a basement which must have pre-dated the Neoclassical building above by several centuries. There were flood marks on the walls hinting that at one time the River Tyburn, which ran beneath our feet, hadn't been quite as tame as it is now.

Backwater hadn't been exaggerating. The place was lined with paper – boxes and folders, from floor to ceiling – and conducting the chaos was the First Lord of the Admiralty himself, stripped to his shirt-sleeves, and not so much supervising his subordinates as chasing them from room to room. From iron-haired lady archivists to young-buck secretaries, there wasn't a man, woman, or rat who didn't squeak and vanish at his approach.

He hailed us, then darted deeper into undercroft, calling for us to follow. We managed well enough, Holmes's long legs making easy work of it while I stumbled after, leaving more of my shin-skin behind than was all-together comfortable.

When we finally caught up with Backwater he was, if possible, even more excitable than before.

"It's happened again, Mr. Holmes!" he exclaimed, red-faced. "About half-an-hour ago. I had instructed my secretary to collect the files on the original investigation and lay them aside for you, but when he opened the safe, they were gone. Yet the strong room is guarded day and night – and nothing else was taken, though there are secrets inside that would fetch a pretty-penny for anyone inclined towards treason." He paused, glanced around in that same way he had at Baker Street, closed the door to our little *oubliette*, and added in a tone terse with excitement, "Not once now, but *twice* – and with such a gap between visits that it seems inconceivable the same person could be involved in both thefts. There's some devilry here!"

Holmes wasted no time in asking to be shown the strong room and Backwater headed off once again, with even Holmes struggling to keep pace.

Given the distance we'd walked, one could imagine that we were now under Parliament itself, only it was quite clear that we'd been led in circles. Backwater's security measures were laughable, but given the man's nervous state, Holmes and I were content to exchange exasperated glances.

We finally arrived at a room lined with cabinets and plan-chests, which boasted a vast iron safe in one corner.

Holmes audibly groaned to see the space, filled as it was with clerks who were in the process of examining every deposit box and every filing cabinet. One elderly lady was carrying boxes piled so high that only her tweed skirt and a pair of floral-patterned shoes were visible. It was something to see her navigate herself out of the room, totally blinded by the ziggurat of paperwork she carried.

"The safe door mechanism is a variation on the Webber and Scott model of 1855," Holmes noted, "requiring two keys to be inserted, simultaneously. Yourself and the guard?"

Newbrook nodded pulling out a large brass key, hanging from a sturdy chain around his neck. "Mine never leaves my person. My secretary has one. And the guards pass theirs to their replacement at their end of their shift."

Holmes asked to examine the keys. I knew from experience that if copies had been made, by pressing some putty or clay into the original, then Holmes's keen eye would spot it.

The secretary and guard both confirmed what Backwater had said. The safe was securely locked and, that morning, had been unlocked using their keys. Once open, the secretary had asked one of the archivists to help find the files. It was then that they discovered it was missing."

"You didn't retrieve them yourself?" Holmes queried.

"I wouldn't know where to begin."

"But you know this archivist?"

"Not personally," the secretary said as though the very suggestion was an affront to his honor.

"Maybe then," Backwater injected, in a tone of palpable frustration, "you could go and find this person?"

The secretary looked quite abashed and vanished into the undercroft, promising to return with the lady in question within a few minutes.

While we waited, Backwater sent the remaining clerks for early lunch, allowing Holmes to began his examination of the strong room. I could see my friend's irritation as he surveyed the chaos in front of him, but he set to work with the same thoroughness as usual.

With his trusty tools – tape measure and magnifying glass – in hand, he trotted noiselessly about the room, pacing and measuring, before finally lying flat upon his face. I saw his hand snake out to grasp something lying in front of a row of deposit boxes affixed to the far wall, then, with a grunt, he was back on his feet.

It seemed that the First Lord of the Admiralty hadn't observed Holmes's furtive motion and it seemed, too, that my colleague wasn't ready to share his discovery.

We made small talk until Backwater's secretary returned, ashen-faced at having been unable to find "the d---ed old woman!", as he put it. Backwater promised to track her down and bring her to our rooms as soon as he located her.

So it was that we wished Backwater a good day and returned to Baker Street.

I was feeling rather deflated when Holmes spun around and, looking strangely animated, grasped me firmly by the shoulders.

"Watson," he said after a moment's pause, "it has long been a belief of mine that it's the little things that are often of most importance. Today, one small thing has proved that axiom to be absolutely correct. You know my methods. You know that I am loathe to reveal my thoughts before all the facts are gathered. I promise you, I will not leave you long in the dark but, for now, I beg that you won't speak to me for a full fifty minutes. This is quite a three-pipe problem."

By the time Holmes emerged from his reverie, I had refilled the lamps and tidied the shelves. He has been true to his word: Less than an hour had passed since he had sat down to ponder the morning's events but, for me, with nothing to do but wait for enlightenment, time crawled. I filled it with a dozen small tasks but, finally, had to content myself with reading the scurrilous scraps of tittle-tattle that passed for news in the pages of the sporting *Pink.*

"First thing's first, Watson," Holmes said without preamble. "What do you make of this?" He held out his hand, and in it, I observed a small, metal *ankh*, about the size of a writing-box key.

"Tantalizing is it not?" Holmes said thoughtfully.

"Egyptian!" I said, remembering Holmes' news clipping. "Coincidence?"

"I refuse to speculate, but I think a telegram to Wilton Crescent may be in order. If there are any family members left in residence, then perhaps they can shed some light on the mysterious Captain Werner."

"Shouldn't we wait on Backwater and the archivist?"

"You know, my dear fellow" Holmes replied mysteriously, "I have a suspicion that they won't have any luck finding that particular 'old woman'."

The weather was cold, but the route pleasant enough for Holmes to suggest we travel on foot. We walked in silence, as men who know each other well often do. It took us half-an-hour at an energetic pace, loitering in Hyde Park long enough to observe the die-hards of the Serpentine Swimming Club break the ice and plunge into London's least-appealing lido.

I know doctors who swear that such things do wonders for all manner of male ailments, but watching all that white flesh turn blue, it seemed that, if we stayed much longer, I'd be required to administer some form of medical assistance.

We walked briskly on until the fifty buildings that form Wilton Crescent came into view. The street curves gently around a tranquil, private garden whose white houses are amongst some of London's most prestigious residences. Number 10 was marked by an imposing black door, and by the time we reached it, we were feeling heavy-footed and ruddy-faced.

Holmes unceremoniously dumped his coat and ear-flapped cap into the butler's outstretched arms. I followed suit.

We were led to a day room furnished with all manner of Egyptian occultism. We were defrosting nicely in front of the fire when an elderly but sprightly lady entered and introduced herself as Susannah Chesters.

The last-surviving daughter of John and Hannah had surely been a handsome young woman. Now in her seventieth year, she looked considerably younger, with flashing green eyes, a winning smile, and an easy manner. She wore a white, ankle-length robe of a type I'd seen sported by Afghani tribesmen. Her hair was covered by a green scarf, presumably chosen to accentuate her eyes. She wore, perhaps, a little too much powder and rouge, but then, even mature ladies must be allowed their vanities.

However, what almost took my breath away was the bracelet hanging about her wrist, which was lined with tiny black *ankhs* that she fingered unconsciously as she spoke. Holmes, curiously, seemed more focused on the lady's shoes, whose dainty floral pattern was certainly appealing, but surely not worth his especial notice.

"Your telegram mentioned my parents?" she began without formalities.

"More specifically about their business partner, Captain Werner," Holmes began.

"Your telegram indicated as much," the lady said. "Something to do with the Admiralty? Please be seated." She waved us towards the wing-backed chairs at either side of the fire. "This will not take long, but you may as well be comfortable. You will no doubt be aware," she said, "that my mother never married the man whose name she took. Please," she added, dismissing my attempts at the social niceties before they'd even been uttered, "this needs to be said. My parents cared deeply for each other, and had my father not already been married – and divorce laws what they are – he would have made things legal. For all that, when a rich, old man takes a young woman for a mistress, she is said to have ruined him. For the latter half of his life, my father was painted as a fool and my mother – worse. For my whole life I, too, have been judged for the perceived sins of my parents. So whatever questions you have, Mr. Holmes, please ask them without judgement."

Susannah spoke with passion but without rancor – something which left me with nothing but admiration for the lady.

"Thank you for you openness, Miss Chesters, but I can assure you," Holmes said with surprising passion, "I have no time for gossip, hearsay, or those who indulge it. My interest lies solely in your parent's business dealings."

Susannah looked at Holmes sharply, in much the same way as I had seen Holmes appraise others in the past. What she saw obviously passed muster, as she flashed him a warm smile and added, "Yes, I can see that you are a singular man,

Mr. Holmes. Not one to be cowed by society. Well then, where to begin?

"My parents would sit where you are sit now," she said, sweeping an arm across the room as though painting the scene. "Werner was here by the window, maps, charts, and notebooks spread across that low table between them. The lamps were lit, and it was in that magical world of shadows and half-seen things that my sisters and I would sit, spellbound."

"Do you recall any specifics?"

Susanna Chesters lit up and suddenly she wasn't an elderly spinster, but someone made young again by the warmth of past memories. "My father followed the work of Monsieur Champollion, who had made such amazing strides deciphering the Egyptian's ancient scripts. He believed that hieroglyphs were the key to the secrets of the ancients. The place where magic and science met. My father loved to speculate and dream. He always saw the possibilities."

Holmes shook his head. "Possibilities?"

"For his work."

"If you don't mind the presumption," Holmes asked, "what was his work?"

"He was an inventor – of sorts. It wasn't widely known, but in certain circles he was known as 'the Great Pharaoh'!"

Holmes fairly bolted upright. "Stage magic?" he asked.

"He fabricated what he called 'ingenious devices' – crafted to appear as arcane machines, passed down through the ages! Many of the greatest magicians owe their success to my father. They paid him handsomely for his ideas and his discretion."

"And Werner?"

"A small man in body and character. He knew my father through the theatre, I believe – they were, at any rate, old friends. At least, until he betrayed them."

"How so?" I asked, increasingly intrigued by the tale now unfolding.

"Father had a mind to set his skills to work for the benefit of the Empire. He had an idea for what he called a 'wave generating machine' which could destroy ships remotely. He began making overtures to the Admiralty. Werner got greedy . . . ."

"There was a falling out?" I hazarded.

"Falling out! Dr. Watson, when – " And here she paused for a moment to collect herself before continuing in a more measured tone. "When my mother learned what Werner had done, she chased him from the house. But by then, it was too late. He had stolen my father's work. Thank the Lord he hadn't the brains to pursue it!"

Her speech – both its intensity and its fascinating subject matter – stayed with us long after we returned to Baker Street.

"But look," I said, "this is all just hocus-pocus. Surely Chesters and Werner were slight-of-hand men. Nothing else to it."

"Indeed?" And how do you explain the *ankh*?"

"Yes! Why didn't you challenge her about that?"

Holmes refused to be drawn further on the subject. Instead he pulled a cigar from the coal scuttle and, lighting it, spent the rest of the evening smoking and staring into the fire. I wasn't party to his thoughts, but mine involved vanishing documents and impossible machines. Sadly, my own poor brain couldn't fathom how the two things were related.

The next morning, Baker Street was still blanketed in snow and, with it, came a strange muffling of sound as though the world was whispering. We were demolishing a pot of hot cocoa when the postman broke the hush. Holmes opened telegram after telegram and, while he didn't deign to share their contents, cries of "Ha!" and "Excellent!" told me that he'd received the information he was after.

I spent the some time kicking my heels while Holmes followed whatever clues his correspondents had led him to. By the time he had throughly satisfied himself, I was eager to rejoin the chase, which led us, of all places, to a mausoleum.

An English funeral is a strange thing indeed. Clocks stopped at the hour of death, mirrors turned to the wall, curtains closed, trails of sable-clad mourners lining the street – and not a women amongst them, in case the drunkenness of that solemn occasion should upset their delicate sensibilities. And, if we are to believe the advertisements put abroad by the funeral peddlers, then there are different qualities of grief according to the social standing of the deceased and the money available to be spent on such public displays.

One will find death in all its variety in London's great cemeteries, yet the places themselves are more like gardens than places of grief. Indeed, thousands visit them for leisure, touring the lanes, and even bringing picnics to share with lost loves, whose new 'homes' proudly boast of their tenant's Earthly accomplishments. "*Here lies George Farthing, late of Cheyenne Mews, business man, magistrate, kind to women, children, and dogs*." And so it goes.

Brompton is perhaps the most beautiful of London's seven formal cemeteries, and it is here that many of the capitol's richest families end their days.

The Chesters' striking mausoleum wasn't hard to find. Though situated in a less fashionable avenue, away from the cemetery's more popular and well-trod paths, it dominated its surroundings.

The structure resembled the doorway of a giant pyramid, if one could imagine that the rest of the monolith had been eroded away by the passage of time. Flat topped, its sides sloping inwards, it was adorned with Egyptian hieroglyphs. There were apparent entrances at all four compass points, but only one – to the west – was marked with a bronze door and had a keyhole.

"Would you not say that this fellow seems to looking directly at the Chesters' mausoleum?" Holmes pointed to a small grave marker, opposite the pyramid, which carried the head of Anubis.

Our miniature deity did indeed seem to be showing a marked interest in its neighbor's resting place.

"Two occupants," Holmes noted, motioning to a pair of hieroglyphic-covered lozenge-shaped cartouches on that grave before turning to view the Chesters' tomb.

There, he handed me one of the telegrams which had arrived at Baker Street earlier in the day. I could see that it came from the cemetery's Management Office and contained a concise reply:

Tomb built 1854. We hold no plans or key.

Holmes rounded on the monument and then, to my unutterable horror, knelt down and pulled a small oilskin bundle from his voluminous pockets. His burglar's tools!

"You can't!" I spluttered.

"I *shouldn't*, perhaps" Holmes replied grimly. "But I *can* and I *will*. And, if you object, then you can do me the favor of watching the path. I have no liking for the work, but logic tells me that what we're looking for is behind this door."

I stayed put and Holmes, glancing back, nodded appreciatively and said in a tone tight with tension, "I knew you wouldn't fail me. Now, hold back, and once I step over the threshold, whatever happens, make no attempt to enter. I may be foolhardy when it comes to my own safety, but I should never forgive myself should anything happen to my dear Watson."

The lock opened with a low click, the door swung open, and I was staring into a tomb so dark that it hurt the eyes to look upon.

Holmes moved to step inside and I was filled with a sense of dread so strong I called out. He looked back at me, his face tight with anxiety. Then, taking a deep breath, he threw the little bundle of burglar's tools to me. "Just in case you need them!" he said, ominously, then stepped over the threshold.

I watched as he turned, looking up, squinting, at something – I knew not what. Then I saw him raise one arm, to touch the far wall. Again, another click, this time from deep within the structure. Holmes stepped briskly backwards.

I heard it as clear as day – an ominous growl deep within the structure. Then there was a magnesium flare, so bright I was forced to look away. My eyes were still adjusting when I heard another click and the door began to swing closed. I looked back just in time to see my friend – Sherlock Holmes – shimmer and vanish into the darkness. The bronze door closed in my face and I was left standing on the steps of that monumental tomb, numb with horror.

I lack Holmes's skills for house-breaking, and it took me quite an hour to find the right combination of picks and torque. I was almost frantic by the time the great door swung open again and I was able to peer inside. The darkness was almost total, and I had to gather my courage before I could persuade myself to enter, dreading what I might find.

The tomb itself exuded an odd scent. Not of decay, as one might expect. More like the earthy odor produced by rain on dry soil. I was relieved to find the floor solid, my first fear being that it had collapsed beneath my friend's feet. Using my cane, I tapped my way across the extent of the vault, but the acoustics were so dampened by the heavy walls and heavy air that if there were any hidden apartments, I couldn't discern them. Next, I worked my way around the walls. Although the structure was little more than a claustrophobic square, it took me another hour to reassure myself that Holmes wasn't trapped within, slumped in an unseen nook.

As I worked my heart pounded, expecting with every step to find Holmes gravely injured – or worse. At the entrance, I noted rows of symbols carved around the edge, in imitation of those on the outside. I girded myself and, standing with my back to the wall, I used the tip of my cane to touch each symbol in turn. I almost expected the floor to descend and carry me into a hidden crypt. I had seen coffin lifts which worked that way, but my hopes were quickly dashed. Finally, in a moment of abject despair, I called out Holmes's name. I repeated it over and over, hearing nothing in return but the dead echo of my own voice.

It was as the day began to fade and the first owls began to emerge from their leafy boughs that I abandoned all hope that Holmes would somehow reappear. I was loathe to call on the police, for this concerned a Government secret. What on Earth would I tell them? But in the end I had no choice. I made my way to the little Porter's Lodge feeling more alone than I had in many years.

In a tomb that clearly wasn't a tomb, I had seen Holmes vanish before my very eyes. I didn't expect the Porter to believe me, but the man's incredulity bordered on the asinine.

I couldn't, of course, admit that we had broken into the mausoleum, and my concern for Holmes' welfare quite sapped my inventiveness. In the end, all I could do was repeat my assertion that Holmes was trapped – maybe dying – and that the fault was his for leaving such a dangerous structure open for anyone to stumble into.

Despite my thinly-veiled accusation, he flatly refused to abandon his post and accompany me to the tomb to resume the search. But I did eventually elicit his promise that he would do so as soon as the Night Porter arrived to start his shift.

So, equipped with a lantern and a blanket, I headed back to the strange pyramid.

The time passed painfully. I examined the tomb two more times, before I admitted defeat, and settled down to wait for the Porter.

Unexpectedly, I dozed, fitfully, dreaming of Holmes trapped and alone, buried alive in some monstrous sarcophagus, clawing at the inside of his gilded tomb with fingers worn to the bone. The scene shifted and I was faced with a giant jackal-headed god, holding a set of scales. On one side lay a feather, on the other my own beating heart. I woke with a start, clutching my at chest, expecting for all the world to find my ribs splintered and my chest hollow.

It was as I pulled myself to consciousness that I realized I could still hear the clawing and gnawing sounds that had inhabited my nightmare!

I grabbed the lantern, and dashed inside the tomb. Its garish light threw up hideous shadows which seemed to dance their way around the walls and, at first, I despaired of seeing anything clearly.

Finally I spotted it! One wall which seemed out of true.

Yes! As I held up the lantern, I could see a gap at the top and – *There!* – the fingers of a hand, pale and much bloodied.

I jammed my own hands into the gap and began to push downwards.

It seemed to take forever but, eventually, I heard that same click I had all those hours ago, and a section of the wall in front of me seemed to fall away into nothing.

Behind it, Holmes' distinctive silhouette emerged. I leapt towards it just in time to catch my friend as he toppled forwards, his face, ashy pale, beads of perspiration upon his brow.

Once safely outside, I wrapped the blanket around Holmes' shoulder and managed to dig out my trusty hip-flask.

He took a dram, looking greatly exhausted, his hands, almost purple with cold, shook as he took it. He downed it in one, and it wasn't until another had been disposed of in the same way that he felt able to speak.

"Watson, I've been a damnable fool, and you may tell me so whenever I take it upon myself to investigate a case without first letting my dear friend in on the secret. If it hadn't been for you, I would, even now, be trapped in some icy morgue, waiting for cold and exhaustion to do their worst."

"But where did you go?"

"Where indeed?" Holmes laughed shortly. "Were I inclined to hyperbole, I would say to Hell and back. Suffice to say, I have been visiting what's left of John Chesters' repository of ingenious devices and ingenious ideas. Thank goodness for penny church candles and a ready supply of matches!"

"You knew?"

"The telegrams gave me my clues. It started with the *ankhs*. We saw them on the bracelet. And, in the clipping, we saw the same design repeated around the door of the tomb. According to the British Museum's Department of Egyptian and Assyrian Antiquities, a common motif in Egyptian art is a pharaoh holding an *ankh*, or passing it on to someone else. The symbolism represents the pharaoh's survival after death. He literally passes his essence into the care of the gods."

I started to wonder how a magician, known as the Great Pharaoh, might interpret that.

"Then there was the fact that, according to Somerset House, the mausoleum was built long before both Hannah and John's deaths. Neither of their daughters were buried in Brompton. So what was it for?"

"John Chesters builds a pyramid to ensure that his 'essence' – his life's work – stays safe?" I asked.

"It would makes sense, especially after the whole Werner debacle." Holmes replied.

"But how was it done?"

"The mechanism was simple enough. You no doubt noted that inside the mausoleum was square. Outside it was pyramidal. I was expecting tricks and hidden compartments. Some sequence linked to the hieroglyphs – a name perhaps – but it turned out that all I needed was a key." He held up the tiny *ankh*.

"Once I had found the key hole, a section of wall slid down to reveal a ladder into the vault below. A little smoke and mirrors added to the theatrical nature of the thing.

"Sadly, time and London weather hasn't been kind to the apparatus. I feared I was trapped there for good." He paused, holding up his bruised and gashed hands, before continuing with ghoulish glee. "There was a point when I believed that I would have to claw my way out of the cold stone surrounding me, inch by inch, but I eventually got the key to turn and, with your help, I ended where I began. I've likely given more than a few cemetery visitors nightmares with my unearthly scrapings and bangings this evening!"

"The Chesters are buried in the small grave opposite?"

"I'm sure that's what the hieroglyphs would tell us, should we go to the effort of translating them."

"The plans!" In all my excitement I had almost lost sight of why we had visited the mausoleum at all. "Were they there?"

Holmes smiled, pulling a mud-smeared bundle of papers from his coat. "Indeed they were!"

We were inching our way towards the North Lodge when the Porter appeared, armed with more blankets, a pick, and a shovel. "Borrowed off-of old Joe, in case push-came-to-shove."

I must admit that my initial impression of the man warmed considerably at his toothy smile and gushing apologies at the sight of my much-abused friend. Doubly so, when he invited us back to the Lodge to share his supper before waving down a cab to take us back to Baker Street.

Once there, I insisted on applying iodine and bandages to Holmes's ragged fingers, but I couldn't compel him to sleep. Instead, he rang for Mrs. Hudson and we indulged in a breakfast of curried Guinea fowl. It's a curious thing that Holmes will go without food for days when a case consumes him but, at its conclusion, will eat with the capacity of a hungry python. I judged from the evident gusto with which he demolished breakfast that we were reaching the end of the chase.

We arrived at Wilton Crescent early enough to have to ring several times before a maid, looking like she had been disturbed in the process of making up the morning's fire, opened the door.

Holmes requested – rather demanded – an interview with Miss Chesters and, despite the girl's protests, we admitted ourselves to the day room to once again await the lady of the house.

We didn't have to wait long. She entered like a whirlwind. "And just who are you," she said in a voice cold and low, "to force your way into my home at this hour?"

Holmes rose, his sharp, eager face, calm and forceful. "I am the man, Miss Chesters, who will not be reporting the theft of secret Admiralty documents to the police. I am the man who will not be handing the culprit over to the authorities. In fact, Miss Chesters I am the man who, at this very moment, is putting his reputation on the line because I believe – as do you – that the device your father proposed is not something that any sane person wishes to see unleashed on the world. But most of all, Miss Chesters, I am the man, who at this moment is your fondest ally."

For a moment the lady said nothing, and then all the tension evaporated from her face. Smiling, she crossed the room and took Holmes's hands in hers. "God bless you, Mr. Holmes! Now, you must have a hundred questions. Please, ask what you will. I know my secrets are safe with you."

Holmes pulled out the bundle of papers he had retrieved from the tomb. "I had occasion to read through these this morning," he said. "See here, Watson: A copy of John Scott Russell's paper on waves of translation. Until his work, such waves really were the stuff of myth and legend. Gigantic waves, generated who knew how, able to sink ships without trace. Your father was able to create these, Miss Chesters?"

"I believe he intended to solicit funds for further research. A machine of the sort he imagined may not even have been possible, but you will see letters to Mr. Russell within, where they discuss their planned collaboration. However, before he could proceed, my father discovered that Werner had contacted the Admiralty independently. He'd arranged some demonstration to convince them that the device had already been made."

"He did sink the hulk?"

She nodded again. "Pure showmanship. Sink shells in the seabed, anchor them under the water, with a long rope attached . . . and with a small submersible to pull the ropes, you can bring the explosive materials together. The explosives do the real damage, but you still generate a wave impressive enough to convince people that some magical wave machine has done the work!"

I laughed then. "So he really did have a submersible?"

"Some remnant of the French wars, I believe."

"Did you steal the plans?" Holmes asked in a half-whisper.

"The Admiralty replaced all of their safes in 1855. My mother kept a weather-eye on such things – waiting for an appropriate opportunity. She was able to take advantage of the chaos to acquire the plans then, much as I did a few days ago.

"Oh, I know now it was a silly risk – but when I got your telegram, I realized the Admiralty wouldn't stop. I had to make sure that all references to that horrible device were destroyed."

With his finger and thumb, Holmes plucked the small black *ankh* he had found in the Admiralty strong room from his waistcoat pocket and handed it to Mrs. Chesters.

"I had missed it. Thank you!" the lady laughed and I noticed, then, how different she looked to our last meeting, without all the powder and rouge. "When I saw you at the Admiralty," she said in answer to my inquisitive looks, "and then later at my house, I feared you would recognize me immediately. Too much powder?"

Holmes chuckled, genuinely delighted. "It was well done! Especially the misdirection with the boxes. Although in truth, it was the distinctive design of your shoes, and not your powder, that gave the game away!"

"It helped having a father who was in the theatre," she replied. "And honestly, Backwater has the place in such an uproar – and so many extra staff – who would notice one more elderly lady? I slipped in with the crowds in the morning, then waited for lunch and left with everyone else. It was no great task to find where the First Lord was, attach myself to his retinue, and make myself quietly invaluable. But Oh! Mr. Holmes, my heart almost stopped when I saw you!"

"You took the papers?"

"Yes, as simple as that!" she said clapping her hands in delight. She leapt up from the chair, and began gathering books from this cabinet and that. "Now, Doctor – how many did I just pick up?"

"Five. No – wait six. You picked up a red leather one. But I don't see it now." I said.

"Very good!" she replied, producing the missing book from under her gown, like a magician producing a rabbit.

"Misdirection. I guessed that someone would be sent to collect the papers. So when Backwater asked his Secretary, all I had to do was follow him to the Vault Room – while making it seem that he was the one following me. Once the safe was open, I palmed the file!"

For a while none of us spoke. Then, without warning, Holmes stood, like a man startled from a deep sleep and turned to Miss Chesters. "Well," he said, "this has been fascinating, but we have already taken up too much of your time. Come Watson."

"But . . . but . . ." I spluttered. "What will you tell the Admiralty?"

"That there's nothing to worry about. That clearly no one would steal such valuable plans and then not use them. That it's all the fault of outmoded bureaucracy. I suspect Backwater will be more than happy not have any more paperwork on the subject."

NOTES

While Watson is, as ever, discrete about his use of real names and places, the Chesters are undoubtedly Hannah and John Courtoy, whose mausoleum is a notable feature of Brompton Cemetery. Their Egyptian-style mausoleum has been the subject of considerable curiosity and speculation over the years. Some even believe that it is transportation chamber or time machine! The details of Hannah Courtoy's life follow much of what Watson records here. She had three daughters out of wedlock with John Courtoy, who was one of London's wealthiest men. No one is certain how he made his fortune.

A small gravestone, said to be designed by Courtoy's great friend, the Egyptologist Joseph Bonomi, is nearby. On it is the head of Anubis, who does appear to look towards the Courtoy mausoleum.

Also buried in Brompton is Samuel Warner, an English inventor of naval weapons, who did indeed demand £200,000 for the plans to "a kind of psychic torpedo" said to be able to destroy ships at great distance. Warner is now regarded as a charlatan. Watson clearly chose to re-name him 'Werner' to save the authorities embarrassment, as the original enjoyed a great deal of support from his friends in parliament.

The weapon trial described did happen and did destroy a hulk, the John O'Gaunt, by unknown means. Plans for the invention were apparently given to the Admiralty, but they have never been found. During a House of Lords inquiry the Duke of Wellington suggested that, as the inquiry was one of a scientific nature, it be entrusted to the Ordnance Department. No report was ever forthcoming.

In 1800, France built a human-powered submarine called the Nautilus. When Warner was questioned by parliament, he is reported to have said that his father, William Warner, had owned the Nautilus, and used it to bring over spies during the Napoleonic Wars. Warner later claimed that he served with his father and used the sub to sink two of the enemy's privateers.

The Nautilus was designed to sink ships using mines which would be attached to the hull of an enemy ship with a spike. As the submarine moved away, a line attached to the device, would pull it into contact with the hull, causing it to explode. The description is similar to Werner's "showmanship" described by Susannah.

In 1834, John Scott Russell described observing waves of translation in a Scottish canal. These waves had long been the subject of maritime myth, but having seen them for himself, Russell speculated that underwater objects could produce waves of vast size, capable of sinking ships with no trace. He was later able to generate these waves under laboratory conditions. Russell's work gave birth to the modern study of solitons. If Courtoy and Russell actually built a machine to generate such waves, it remains 'lost'.

The Singular Case of Dr. Butler

"Well, I'm not sure Mrs. Hudson would approve of smoked haddock for supper," Holmes said as he pushed his empty plate across the kitchen table with a satisfied air, "but I'd call that a very fair effort for a gentleman in such straitened circumstances."

"Straitened indeed!" I exclaimed in mock indignation although, if truth were based on appearances alone, his comments would seem justified.

It had been a month since the maid had moved to Devonport with her fiancé, who was training at HMS Vivid. The housekeeper had followed suit and departed for the family farm in Clwyd. And Mrs. Watson had, with some gentle persuading, vanished a week ago to help her niece with the new baby. As for me? Now that my dearest was safely away from the bombs, I'd rather reverted to type. With the house closed up, I'd turned the kitchen into a neat little billet – one room being so much easier to heat and clean. War had made us all reassess our priorities, and while I missed my wife terribly, I found that such simple living suited me exceptionally well.

"And how is Mrs. Watson?" Holmes asked with a replete yawn.

"Worried. The Zeppelin raids ..." I left the rest unfinished.

"And you? Now you're back in harness, I hope you're giving the new generation of RAMC doctors Hell."

I'd been volunteering at the Queens and, while it's true that a bullet wound is still a bullet wound, the injuries inflicted by mustard gas, hand-bombs, and flamethrowers had plunged me nose-deep into my books. There was so much to learn about all the new ways of killing. "It's like being an intern again," I groaned, "only I don't recall wanting to sleep quite so much the first time around. In all honestly, I'm not sure how much use an old sweat like me is going to be to the war effort."

"Nonsense Watson! I hear your lectures are eagerly attended."

"Oh?" I replied, with a flush, unaware that Holmes had been following my career so closely. "Well, of course, I did used to be *The* Dr Watson."

"You'll always be the definitive article to me, dear fellow," Holmes chuckled cordially.

"And you?"

Holmes gave me the whisper of a smile. "Mycroft has been keeping me busy."

I felt a spark of adrenaline and yes, a little jealousy. Knowing that Holmes was out playing The Great Game without me reminded me how much things had changed. And how much we had changed, too.

It was true that Holmes looked little different, but I for one was feeling my age, and happy to admit it.

"Then Watson, it's only fair that I attempt the washing up." He leapt up with one if his characteristic bursts of energy. "Now, while I do battle here," he said, tying on an apron, "perhaps you'll tell me what you know about this Butler business. He was a House Man at the Queen's was he not?"

"Indeed. Before the war. Then, in August, he rejoined us to complete his training. Poor chap had a rough time of it at the Somme. In hospital for almost six months, but still determined to do his bit. He has the makings of a damn fine doctor too."

"That was before he emptied his revolver into this Peterson fellow… ."

"Yes. Frightful affair. I know Scotland Yard has agreed to take a back-seat while you make discrete enquiries, but this sort of thing is terribly bad for moral. Has the whole university on edge."

"You've already spoken to the coroner, have you not? What were his findings?"

"Grim. Peterson was shot three times, at close range. One shot to the chest, one to the neck, the other grazed the right temple. Peterson likely tried to pull the gun away from Butler – hence the arrangement of the shots. Whatever happened, though, Butler did the poor chap a favor. His body was riddled with cancer."

"Now, that is interesting," exclaimed Holmes. "Butler definitely fired the shots? It was Peterson who grabbed Butler's gun, and not the other way around?"

"There aren't many suicides who try to shoot themselves in the chest, if that's what you're suggesting." I held out an imaginary gun out to demonstrate the logistics. "Besides, Butler would surely have said something. Yet the only words he's spoken since the shooting seem to imply his guilt."

"No weapon was found at the scene?"

"None."

"And the official explanation for that?"

"It was cleverly hidden, and will turn up."

"And what does the rumor-mill have on it? "Holmes asked, thoughtfully.

"That Peterson had been seeing a little too much of Butler's wife. Frankly, that's rot. Peterson and Butler came up together, and there's never been so much of a sniff of impropriety. "

"He's currently in Broadmoor?"

"Quite so. His doctor cited war-neurosis and he's awaiting assessment. But, as I say, he steadfastly refuses to speak to anyone."

"Even *The* Doctor Watson?"

"Even *The* Doctor Watson."

Holmes finished the dishes in silence and returned to the little pitted kitchen table with a familiar gleam in his eyes.

"What do you think, Watson? Could your students spare you for a few days?"

"Indeed," I replied as that old familiar thrill began to surface. "Term ended on Friday. I have three weeks break before lectures restart in the New Year."

"Well then," Holmes said, tamping the tobacco into his pipe with infinite care, "it would seem that the game's afoot!"

The next day, London had donned its winter garb. My basement billet was a gloomy place at the best of times, but this morning the sun had barely risen, and the wind screamed against the little barred casement window like some untamable beast fighting for ingress.

I'd sent a telegram early, utilizing the ever-growing network of small boys that seem to haunt these war-torn streets.

Sid – my usual factotum – couldn't have been more than fourteen but told me with great dignity that he'd soon be taking the King's shilling and would have to pass my business along to another of his crew. I'd known boys in Afghanistan who'd been enraptured by the fiery words of the recruiting officers and lied about their age to go to war. But Sid had a strange zeal about him that made me feel both proud and afraid. So much so, that as I tended the fire, I drifted into a kind of waking dream in which the medical illustrations I'd been pouring over took on the guise of young Sid, so horribly mutilated that even his own mother would struggle to recognize him.

I furiously stoked up the range and, by the time Holmes materialized, I was hunkered in front of it like some wild man of yore, staring into the flames, trying to keep the monsters at bay.

In place of a dressing gown Holmes had a blanket draped, like some monkish habit, across his spare form. So comical was the sight that it immediately shook me from my funk.

"My dear fellow!" I exclaimed as my friend noisily stretched the knots out of his gaunt frame, "you really must let me open up one of the bedrooms for you."

He'd spent the evening camped in the study, with his long form unfeasibly folded into my battered Turkish arm chair. "Not at all, my dear Watson. I was able to make myself a cozy nest amongst your books and nick-nicks. Besides," he added, with an impish grin, "I think the calico is rather fetching."

We made a lazy breakfast, in very much the bachelor mode of things: whatever left-overs needed our attention, washed down with copious amounts of steaming Arabian coffee.

"I've taken the liberty," I began, "of telegramming Mrs. Butler – "

"Capital!" Holmes said in that high tone which was often the only hint of the excitement bubbling beneath an otherwise calm exterior. "Shall we go on foot? I've a mind to see what the city has been doing with herself in my absence."

The great metropolis had indeed been busy in the years since Holmes had retired from the business of knowing other people's business.

Signs of war were everywhere. Posters of Lord Kitchener's face alongside the words "*Wants You!*" were emblazoned on the side of every omnibus. Bomb damage was apparent on both Exeter and Wellington Streets. Uniformed men from all over the Empire came and went. Yet it was the small changes that were perhaps the most revealing of the national mood. Butchers' shop windows now advertised luncheon sausage rather than German sausage. The King of Prussia pub had been renamed in honor of the King of Belgium. Wiesbaden Road had become Belgrade Road. Everywhere Teutonic names and their holders were being expunged. I recalled with a shudder the report of an Austrian couple, recently married and only in their twenties, who took poison from fear of internment and separation. West London had thankfully escaped the horrible anti-German rioting of Canning Town and West Ham, but everywhere we walked we saw fear and distrust in the faces of those we passed.

We walked in silence for the most, Holmes's cool grey eyes seeming to catalogue and analyze each new detail.

The Butler's residence proved to be a surprisingly modest but delightful two-up-two-down with its own rose-garden and space out back for children and chickens. Both could be heard making their own distinctive cluckings as we approached.

Such homes had once been common in London but now seemed out of place in this burgeoning twentieth-century city. "A bit like ourselves, Holmes?" I opinioned.

"Indeed," he replied, clearly amused. "Neat, well proportioned, vintage, but holding up well against the press of time. Unless of course you were talking about the chickens?"

I was swallowing a guffaw when the door was opened by a woman with doe-eyes, a worn smile, and a profusion of inky hair that clearly defied any attempts at being tamed. She ushered us into the small parlor, and to a pair of sturdy chairs, set around a cheery hearth. Despite the chill, the French Windows were ajar. There, as we'd surmised, was a neat little kitchen garden, in which twins were patiently supervising a flock of chickens pecking for grubs amongst the last of the winter vegetables.

"We did have apartments near the hospital," she began, embarrassed at the spartan simplicity of the surroundings. "Then Joseph went up to the front, and a soldier's pay isn't large, and help became so hard to find," she trailled off before adding whistfully "and I had this crazy idea that roses would somehow make it all the more bearable."

"Even the most beautiful rose still has it thorns," Holmes replied quietly.

"Oh! How true!" she gasped, quite jumping from her seat and grasping Holmes's hand with a sudden rush of emotion. "If only you knew!"

"Why don't you tell us? I can assure you, we have only your husband's best interests at heart," Holmes said in that tone he has that seems to install instant confidence.

"I cannot! Believe me Mr. Holmes when I say I cannot." As she spoke she glanced at the children playing so contently amongst the rows of kale and leaks. "I dare not."

"Dare not?"

"War changes a man," was all she could be compelled to say and Holmes quickly shifted his line of questioning.

"What can you tell me of Peterson, then? Is there any reason your husband would have wanted to kill him?"

Mrs. Butler resumed her seat, her eyes holding Holmes's with a desperate intensity. "If you're asking if I gave him cause to be jealous – no, Mr. Holmes. Never. Any jealousy that existed came from David – Mr. Peterson – alone. We were close, we three, growing up and although it was never spoken of, David always felt he was the better man. He begrudged Joe his successes, yet was happy to take what windfalls that brought. It was my husband who recommended him for his post at the Queen's. But my husband was – Joseph is – the most gentle and trusting of men and he could never find any fault in his old friend."

"And … forgive me … but did Peterson ever seek to win your affections?"

"Both courted me, but I believe David never quite forgave me from choosing Joe over him. When Joe was sent to the front, I felt it prudent to never be alone with him. I make no accusations, you understand, but people do talk so."

"And now that your husband has returned?"

She spoke slowly, all the time twisting her wedding band around her finger like a rosary, whose every revolution represented some silent prayer of contrition. “He paid me a visit a few days after Joseph returned to his duties. I thought it best not to invite him in and things become somewhat heated. After that, Joseph and he were … not unfriendly. No, not that, but things were strained.”

Holmes leaned forward, steepling his fingers, pensively. “And what else can you tell us of Peterson? His personality?”

“Quick to anger. A grudge-bearer. Even my husband would have acknowledged that, and they were the dearest of companions.”

The clock on the mantle ticked away the minutes and for a while Holmes was shipwrecked in thought. Then, in a blink, he was back.

“Just a few more questions Mrs. Butler but I fear these will be difficult for you.”

She nodded and, as she did so, I saw a steely resolve grow upon her. “Joseph’s life is on the line. What are my feelings compared to that? Ask your questions, Mr. Holmes.”

“When he returned from the front, was your husband much changed?”

She started then, and when she spoke those huge eyes were flecked with tears. “More than you could know. But not in the ways that mattered. No, although it took me some time to realize that for myself. Not in the ways that mattered.”

“You mentioned that Peterson and he were not as close as they had been. What of the children? How were they towards him?”

"Well, they are young and have been without their father for almost eighteen months. They barely remember him. That's a blessing in a way. Still," she added with a sad smile, "when this terrible business is over, I pray they will have plenty of time to get to know Joseph properly."

The day was one of gun-metal clouds and dreary drizzle as Holmes and I struck out for the Underground. Traveling on the two-penny tube, as it's popularly known, may indeed be a form of modern torture, but it is thankfully speedy. It took us less than ten minutes to reach Hampstead and from there, we headed to The Queen's Free Teaching Hospital.

I lead Holmes to the tennis courts at the rear of the main building, where vast army surplus tents had been erected to serve as emergency field hospitals. A quick check at the nurses' station gave us the information we required, and soon we were introducing ourselves to Helena Browning of Queen Alexandra's Imperial Military Nursing Service.

I have often felt that nursing is pitiless and unpleasant work. Many of the young woman now are volunteers, of course. They have the confidence that a middle class education brings, but are totally unsuited to the realities of the profession. Trained nurses are a different type entirely. Some doctors still treat them as little more than domestics, but I've found them to be an admirable breed.

Miss Browning seemed impossibly young for such responsibilities. She looked beyond tired, but fuelled by genuine passion for the job. She was chaperoned by an elderly lady who didn't introduce herself, but instead lurked in the background like the proverbial ghost at the feast.

"Honestly, sirs," Miss Browning began anxiously, her words spilling out all of a rush, "I'll tell you what I know, but it's precious little." Knowing that a nurses' terms of service could be revoked for the slenderest reasons, I understood her anxiety and quickly got to the meat of the matter.

"I believe you were the first on the scene at the shooting of Dr. Peterson?"

"I was. Poor man. But he was already beyond any help I could have given."

"There's no question of blame, Miss Browning. We merely want to know what happened."

"Thank you, sir!" she said, clearly revealed. "My understanding is that Dr. Peterson had asked Dr. Butler to meet him in the arboretum. As the resident anesthesiologist, he wanted to discuss the possibility of providing each tent with its own nitrous oxide supply."

"Why Dr. Butler? He's a Junior. And surely Manners deals with procurement?"

"I'm sure I don't know, sir."

"Who told you this?"

"Why, Dr. Peterson himself."

"Please if you will," Holmes, interjected "talk me, through the train of events, Miss Browning. Omit no detail, no matter how trivial it may seem."

"Right you are, sir. This was Tuesday morning, last. Matron had asked me to check on supplies of bandages, so I was heading towards the North Stairs. Suddenly Dr. Peterson appeared – as if from thin air. The hallway is always ill-lit and he gave me such a shock. For a moment, all I saw was his white coat and I thought I'd finally seen old Headless Henry himself! Silly really, but there seemed to be something in the air that day. I swear I was as jumpy as hungry dog.

"I was about to head on when he stops me for the time. That was strange because he had a fine old pocket watch on a chain on his waistcoat. Well, I says, 10.05, and he gives a little intake of breath and looks at me, nervously. Honestly, sir, the more I think about it, the more I wonder if he didn't had some horrible premonition of what was about happen, because he looked like the Grim Reaper himself was tapping him on the shoulder."

"Helena!" The ejaculation – coming from the unnamed woman – was parade-ground sharp with an edge of threat. "No more of your nonsense now. I've told you before about letting your fancies run away with you. I won't have these gentlemen thinking my nurses are flighty, over-excitable things."

Holmes held up a placating hand, "Madam, if you will allow Miss Browning to continue, I can assure you that any and all impressions, no matter how fanciful they may seem, may be of inestimable value. Women in general, and nurses in particular, often have strong intuitions which I've found that it pays to respect."

Somewhat mollified, the Matron nodded for Miss Browning to continue which, not withstanding the rebuke, she did at the same breakneck speed and in the same the flighty and over-excitable tone.

"As I say, he looked a little strained, and he tells me that he's meeting Dr. Butler at 10.30, and if I should see him first, would I hurry him along."

"And did you see him?"

"I did, Sir. At 10.27, walking down the steps from the rear entrance, so I delivered my message."

"That's very precise."

The nurse looked down at her fob watch, which was pinned to the top of her cape. "Yes, sir. In this job, you always have to have one eye on the time."

"And where was Peterson?" Holmes asked.

"I couldn't see him, but I noted Dr. Butler heading towards the arboretum. And it was then that I saw *her* too."

"Her?"

"The Angel of Mons, Mr. Holmes! All translucent white and floating. She pointed. "Right there – above the tree line. I know how it sounds, sir, and I've been told not to speak of it. But I'll take the Bible on it! I saw her as clearly as I see you."

The pronouncement was so unexpected that both Holmes and myself were momentarily stunned.

When Holmes spoke again, it was with deliberate care. "You saw an angel?" he asked.

Miss Browning nodded sheepishly.

My friend raised an eyebrow quizzically, just the whisper of a smile crossing his lips. "And then you heard the shots?"

"Yes, sir. Two, maybe three, but so close together it was hard to tell. Followed by an awful cry – enough to chill the blood."

"When did this happen?"

"Not long after 10.30."

"How long after? Be as accurate as you can."

"Maybe two minutes."

"You didn't check your watch?"

"No, sir. I was too busy running."

"And when you got to the arboretum, what did you see?"

"Lord, it was terrible! Dr. Peterson was on his back. His hands on his chest – sort of twitching. So much blood. And Dr. Butler standing over him."

"Did you speak to Butler?"

"I did. I asked him what had happened and he said 'That's all for me! I'm done for!' Then 'Kate – Lord – Kate!'"

"Kate is Mrs. Butler?"

"I believe so."

"What do you think he meant?"

Miss Browning clearly had very definite ideas about what was meant, but chose the better part of valor and remained silent.

The interview concluded, Holmes set off like a greyhound out of a trap, fairly vibrating with the need for action. By the time I'd caught up with him in the arboretum he was nose to the ground, lens poised. "As I thought," my friend sighed, clambering up with more elegance than my old legs would have managed. "The Yard's resident ballet troop have already done their *temps levé* all over the arena."

He continued to survey the scene, pacing swiftly across the grass, his head sunk upon his chest. "Hullo!" he shouted. "Watson, what do you make of this?"

He pointed to a deep, rounded indentation, which even the press of feet and inclement weather hadn't managed to erase. "Not an angel, I'd hazard," he said, with a flash of dry humor.

"No, nor Headless Henry,!" I replied in kind. "Certainly something heavy." Remembering Peterson's field of expertise, I had a sudden inspiration. "Some type of gas receptacle?"

"Exactly! And look here … ." Holmes pointed to a lighter patch of grass indicating that something had been dragged across the lawn. He followed the trail, plunging into the undergrowth, and emerging with a glass cylinder of the type used in a Gwathmey Device.

The little valve on the top had been left open. It was quite empty, with no way of telling what gas it might have originally contained.

"For anesthesia?" Holmes queried.

"Something of the type, but Peterson was the expert I'm afraid. It's such a new field – only included in curriculum six years ago. It's not nitrous oxide, though. That comes in a metallic cylinder."

He continued to prowl the grounds, his quick eyes darting their questioning glances. He seemed particularly fascinated by the direction in which the trees had been bent by the wind, which tended to be channeled by the buildings east-west.

Then, for a full fifteen minutes, he had me time him walking from the steps to the arboretum.

"What do you make of it Watson? Four minutes. Two more for Miss Browning to deliver her message. If her statement is accurate, Butler barely had time to speak to Peterson at all."

"Should I have been the outraged lover, I would certainly have had some heated words with my rival, before gunning him down." I replied.

"Indeed!" Holmes smiled. "You know Watson, I'm starting to think that we may have been here before."

"Whatever do you mean?"

In place of a reply, Holmes nodded towards the Jacobean tower that formed the grand feature of the hospital's central building. "Are you up for a little clamber?" he grinned mischievously.

I barely had time to register my surprise before Holmes was once again off on the chase. I eventually caught up with him at the bottom of the wooden staircase which winds, round and up, to a worm-ridden platform that allows for maintenance of the clock.

Holmes didn't even pause, his long-legged stride taking two, sometimes three steps, at a time. For myself, I was content to test each stair as I came to it, clinging for dear life to the banister, as the whole structure wobbled and groaned under our combined weight. There were many times during that climb that I cursed the luck of having a friend who cares naught for his own safety.

I was winded and panting hard by the time I reached the last of the eight-hundred-forty steps and gingerly stepped up onto the wooden platform. I was just in time to see Holmes vanish onto the balcony that runs around the circumference of the tower. I heard the clatter of falling masonry and, when I stepped out, Holmes was heaving himself onto balustrade. He stood on tip-toe, while I watched, hardly daring to breathe, his long pale fingers stretching out towards something seemingly entangled on the arrow-head of the hour hand.

Holmes shifted his weight, trying to gain a few precious inches, his feet now perilously close to the edge. I saw him pluck at something, and his hand move to secure it. But the guardrail was too narrow, the balusters too worn. Every movement, every twist of his body made the structure shift and grind. I had a sudden foreboding of impending danger – then – it happened. The hour hand shifted and Holmes fell.

I saw it all in slow-motion. One moment I was watching his feet slide off the guardrail, the next I was hanging over the stone parapet, my hands clasped around Holmes's wrist with sixty feet of daylight and stone yawning below.

To this day I have no idea how I managed to cover the distance between us so quickly. Nor do I recall the moment when my hand grasped his. I do know that I clutched at air and cloth for what seemed like an eternity and that, when Holmes's startled eyes met mine, I felt the strength of a much younger man flood my body. No – this was not to be how the great Sherlock Holmes, my oldest and dearest friend, was to end his days.

Slowly, inch by painful inch, I began to haul Holmes back from the brink. Several times he slipped. Several times I felt the cramped balcony beneath us protest at its ill-usage. Once, in an effort to get greater leverage, I almost toppled over guardrail myself and ended cursing roundly at the pulled muscles and the closeness to disaster.

When Holmes was finally safe, we lay propped against the rough brick of the clocktower too weary to move despite the precariousness of our situation.

Holmes eventually broke the silence. "My dear Watson," he said contritely, "it seems there is simply no teaching this old dog new tricks! My mind, I fear, is too often absorbed with the problem ahead and too rarely concerned with the perils of the moment! Still," and here he began to chuckle, "we can at least return to Queen Anne Street with a fitting memento of today's near-death experience."

From his pocket he pulled the remains of a make-shift balloon, its white, silken cloth much torn and muddied. Strings dangled from the bottom of the envelope and, from one of them hung a Webley revolver with the initials *DP* elegantly carved into the hilt.

"Gracious!" I cried. "Peterson's gun."

"And," Holmes said with a glint in his eye, "Miss Browning's angel!"

That evening, Holmes and I retired to the study to contemplate the day's discoveries. We sat on either side of the fireplace as we had done so many times before and, for a moment, I could have fancied that we were indeed back in our old digs in Baker Street.

"So it was suicide, then?" I said, unwilling to break the spell, but keen to hear my friend's thoughts all the same."

"It would appear so. Let me lay out the train of events for you, and see how they stand. Peterson sets up this meeting with Butler. He waits in the hallway for a passing nurse – our Miss Browning – and ensures that she knows he's meeting Butler, where and when. Presumably he'd already secured the cylinder of helium or hydrogen and hidden the ballon in the undergrowth. A simple matter, then, to inflate it and wait for Butler to arrive. There were three shots. The first was the *coup mortel*. Peterson held the gun at arm's length, directed at his heart, just as you demonstrated. The others? We cannot know until we've spoken to Butler, but it seems likely that, seeing what his friend intended he attempted to prevent it. The balloon then carries away the gun, which we now know could clearly be identified as Peterson's. He couldn't have bought another, unmarked one, without a license – hence the rather ingenious method of its disposal. Enter Miss Browning to hear Dr Butler's apparent confession. But what is missing?"

"Why?"

"Yes!" Holmes said, with a burst of excitement. "Why would a dying man arrange his own death in such a way to implicate someone who was once his dearest friend?"

"*Cherchez la femme*?" I hazarded.

"No, it won't do. Peterson's affection for Mrs. Butler not withstanding, they were once the best of friends. Something changed. Something so dramatic that Peterson could not let it go."

"War changes a man."

"Mmm. I do wonder … ." I could see Holmes's eyes take on that faraway look which bespoke of furious mental activity. I re-filled our glasses with a healthy shot of malt and sat back to watch the fire burn down as, once again, Holmes was lost to me in the mist of his own thoughts.

Crowthorne is a curious place. A picturesque English village which houses both the grand Rococo buildings of one of our nation's most prestigious public schools and the rather more forbidding walled enclosure of Broadmoor Hospital for the Criminally Insane.

The previous day, Holmes had packaged up the remnants of Peterson's ballon along with a note to Butler assuring him of our sympathy to his cause. Within the hour, we'd received a call from Broadmoor informing us that Butler had broken his silence – and requested our presence.

Although we'd telephoned ahead to arrange passes, in such secure environs, the name of the great consulting detective held little sway. We were compelled to cool our heels for almost half an hour while our identities were confirmed. Then, a square-set guard granted us access to the first of many sets of locked and barred doors.

Despite all the security, Broadmoor is not a prison but a hospital, although many of its patients have committed such heinous crimes in their madness that the place has a tangible air of threat. Its corridors are long and cheerless, echoing, as they do, with the cries of the demented and distressed. Their bone white walls and pitiless lighting adds to the effect of a place utterly devoid of human warmth. It is not a place that I ever want to re-visit.

Butler's cell proved to be a simple square, padded to prevent self-harm. A set of iron anchor rings were set into the wall. Fortunately, Butler was not considered a risk either to himself or others and we were spared the necessity of conducting our interview with him in chains.

While my previous attempts to speak to Butler had been roundly rebutted, this morning he seemed a changed man. He greeted us warmly, his eyes filmy with tears, his voice shaking with emotion.

He looked, in truth, stretched thin. His eyes were large and expressive with a wide, haunted mien. His face was pale and handsome, although pocked with the scars characteristic of the *bullae* that result from exposure to mustard gas. The result was quite arresting.

"Doctor! Mr. Holmes!" he said, his voice momentarily breaking. "Your message gave me such hope!"

"But good heaven's, man!" I cried. "Why didn't you speak up before?"

"I had not expected to be believed. It was all so fantastical . . . ."

"But had the police heard your story, they would have searched the grounds, as Holmes did. The proof of your innocence was hidden in plain sight!"

"I think," Holmes said, slowly, "that there is more to this than you are want to admit, is that not true Dr. Butler?"

"What could you possibly mean?" Butler licked his lips, and for a moment despair clouded his features again.

"Dr. Butler, once I give my report, you will be a free man. But make no mistake, the extraordinary circumstances of Peterson's death will raise questions. I can help satisfy the authorities, but I need you to trust me. I know you fear an investigation. Clearly, you felt that it was better to be locked away here" – Holmes waved his hands expansively – "then have the truth revealed. Mrs. Butler herself has given me the bones of it. She spoke of her husband, 'Joe', in the past tense but 'Joseph' in the present tense. So I know that you have kept quiet, not for yourself but for her sake, and that tells me you are a man deserving of every aid I can give."

"Very well," Butler said softly. "What I tell you now will no doubt sound impossible but I ask you to listen without prejudice and accept that everything I say is the absolute truth.

"My name is Joseph Bueller, Captain, Eighth Division, Regiment 72 of the Imperial German Army. I was born, and I spent my first fifteen summers in London. When my mother –

who was an English woman – died, my father returned us to Germany.

"At the outbreak of war, I was in the final year of my medical studies. By then, my Englishness was becoming a burden to my father. Rather than see him interred or further shamed, I did what was required to prove my patriotism. I abandoned my studies and went off to fight an enemy who I felt more kinship towards than I did for my own people.

"I went to war in the Autumn of 1914. By 1916, I was but twenty-five-years-old, and already a veteran, with more friends beneath the soil than above it. Yet although I have seen horrors that will stay with me until I am old and grey, I can barely speak of the Somme. I can not talk to you, coldly and rationally, of tactics, of battles, troop movements, of the whens and the hows. The Somme to me is not a place. Not a battle. It is an abode of madness. The mouldering dead, the snarling of carrion dogs, the endless thunder of the guns, the cries of the dying. For months, we existed in this grey desert of death. Never fully sleeping, never fully waking, staggering through the days with fear like a rat gnawing at our guts. Until, finally, the day came that I had been both dreading and longing for, and I was sent over the top.

"I think only those who have been in battle will know the strange calm that descends on you as you head out to die. Through the mud, through the gas, through the smoke of belching ordnance, I ran. I did not see the face of the enemy, rather I felt my gun buck, felt steel clash against steel, steel enter flesh. I fought with a hollow emptiness at my centre. There was no glory, no adrenaline, no thill. Only fire, move, thrust. Move, fire, thrust. Blood, and pain, and the terrified eyes of children locked with mine, as they gasped their last breath. On and on, until I thought I would go mad with it.

"Then, I saw a light, bright and burning on the horizon. I felt my chest scald and my skin singe, followed by blackness. When I came to, the battle had moved on, and the cool air of approaching night brought a semblance of clarity to my thoughts. The shell had, I think, thrown me some distance. I had landed hard enough to break several ribs, my legs, and my shoulder blade. I was bleeding from a dozen wounds, concussed and naked, but half buried in mud which gave me a peculiar sort of warmth and comfort.

"I looked around and beside me was a British officer – a captain like myself. It was when he turned to look at me that I decided I had indeed gone mad. For here was my very twin. Oh, I had the marks of mustard gas on my face, and his features were fuller, less sharply defined. But for all that, my twin!

"We lay there for two days and two nights. He slowly dying from a stomach wound, myself unable to do more than lie beside him. As we learnt of each other, the madness of our situation only increased. We were both junior doctors, both named Joseph – although he preferred to be called Joe. Both of us had chosen the life of a simple soldier rather than have our ease as a doctor in some sterile dressing station. We spoke of this and much more, each with the growing fancy that maybe we were cousins from some long lost branch of the family tree. Even my surname, Bueller, is so similar to Butler, is it not?

"He spoke of his family, and it was then that he made me promise that, should I live, I would find his wife and tell her what had become of him. He died within the hour, and I took his tags determined to keep my promise to a man I had come to think of as a brother.

"On the third day, as far as I could figure it, a fever began to take me. I lost time, I lost my place in the world. I drifted, no longer in pain – ready to join the great unknown. But Providence had other plans. The next thing I knew, I was in a British army hospital, with tear-stained letters by my bedside from Butler's wife telling me about our children and how she was counting the days until we could be reunited.

"I had determined, Mr. Holmes, not to deceive her, but neither did I want the censors to read my letters and become aware of the truth before I could fulfill my promise. So when I was well enough I wrote back, but in such a way that she would know that things were not as they appeared. You can not imagine what it was like for Kate that day, to open the door to a stranger with her husband's face. She bore it bravely – and my resolve hardened.

"I had devised a plan where I would sign over all my – Butler's – goods and chattels to her then quietly disappear. But, as the days moved on it became clear to me that I didn't just share Butler's face, I shared his love for his wife. At first I dared not speak of it. Dared not hope. But truth was our beacon, and at the end of two weeks she told me that she too had begun to see me, not as a stranger but as a second chance for happiness. That, dear Lord, she loved me too!"

"But Peterson suspected?" Holmes asked in a half-whisper.

"From the beginning. My voice ... my mannerisms ... he knew me from childhood. Finally, Kate was free to be his, but instead she had chosen me. This *doppelgänger*! It made him quite crazed, I think. He went to Kate and threatened to tell the whole world that she'd taken a stranger – an enemy soldier – into her bed … unless. Well, you can imagine what the price of his silence was to be.

"She told him he was crazy, that no one would believe such nonsense. And it was true. He knew that, and it ate away at him. For my part, I kept up the pretense, schooled by Kate in the minutest details of our shared childhood. I think that's when he set upon his plan. If he couldn't have her, then he would make sure I couldn't either."

Bueller finished his tale with the look of a man glad to have finally been confessed. He seemed almost reborn, his eyes, so full of emotion, gleaming with contentment and hope for the future.

As we walked back to the station, I turned to Holmes and asked what he would do next. I had often accused my friend of being something of a cold fish, but I knew that a keen sense of fairness burned within him and he would not fail the young couple.

"Everything in my power!" he said. "Scotland Yard will be happy to have one less case to deal with in these difficult times. Nor will they want to let the press run wild with tales of angels and bizarre deaths, which would certainly damage the hospital's reputation. No, I think they will follow my advice and report it as a simple suicide."

He paused for a moment taking a deep breath of the cool afternoon air, like a man surfacing from some deep pool in which he has too long been immersed. "Come, Watson, I think we have earned this evening's repast. I hope Simpson's hasn't been hit too hard by rationing?"

"Not too badly at all," I replied, linking Holmes's arm, in the way that old comrades do. "Not too badly at all."

Epilogue

In recording these events, I beg the critics not write and tell me that there is no such hospital, no such personages, or that, in fact, that I could not be in one place when I had previously written I was in another. It has often been my habit when recording cases involving my remarkable friend, to alter certain names and dates to save those involved further heartache, should some keen-eyed reader put two two together and naturally come to four. However, the details – miraculous as they seem – were as I have written. I am delighted to report that Joseph and Kate "renewed" their vows to one another not a week after his release from Broadmoor. They now live very quietly in civil practice where the family are considered, by all who know them, to encapsulate everything worth fighting for in this great nation of ours. And you have the word of *The* Dr. Watson on that.

John H. Watson, M.D, December, 1917.

NOTES

There was no WW1 equivalent of the Blitz, but bombs dropped by Zeppelins and heavy bi-planes were a genuine source of terror in the capitol. The last bomb attack of the war, in October 1917, saw seven 300-pound bombs released on London when a Zeppelin crew, heading for the industrial north, were blown off course and disorientated by altitude sickness. This is likely the attack that prompted Watson to send his wife to stay with relatives.

In his determination to protect Butler's identity, Watson has blended two hospitals. The first is the Royal Free University Hospital, which was a famous teaching hospital on the Gray's Inn Road. This served as a military hospital for officers during the latter stages of WW1. The second is Chase Farm hospital in Enfield, which has a noted clock tower.

It wasn't until 1912 that anesthetics were included in the curriculum of all British medical schools. When Britain entered WW1, on 4th August 1914, anesthesia as we think of it today was largely non-existent in battle-field situations. The military finally created specialist anesthetic posts in 1916 in response to the appalling number of injured soldiers dying from pain and shock. The standard Gwathmey-Woolsey Nitrous Oxide-Oxygen Apparatus (developed in 1912) held two cylinders of nitrous oxide and one of oxygen. Nitrous oxide and oxygen came in metal cylinders with a glass "bubble bottle" to control the mix. Presumably Peterson adapted this bottle to fill his make-shift ballon.

Queen Alexandra's Royal Army Nursing Corps is the nursing branch of the British Army. Matron holds the equivalent rank of Major.

Milton Keynes UK
Ingram Content Group UK Ltd.
UKHW020736140424
440967UK00012B/84/J